Chrissa

by
Mary Casanova

American Girl®

For every girl who finds her voice and makes a difference

Published by American Girl Publishing, Inc.
Copyright © 2009 by American Girl, LLC

Questions or comments? Call 1-800-845-0005,
visit our Web site at americangirl.com, or write to Customer Service, American Girl, 8400 Fairway Place, Middleton, WI 53562-0497.

Printed in China
09 10 11 12 13 14 LEO 12 11 10 9 8 7

All American Girl marks and Chrissa™, Chrissa Maxwell™, Sonali™, and Gwen™ are trademarks of American Girl, LLC.

Illustrations by Richard Jones

Special thanks to Patti Kelley Criswell, MSW, Dr. Michael Obsatz, and Susan Kovacs

Cataloguing-in-Publication Data available from the Library of Congress.

Contents

1

Parallel Universe

The yellow bus wheezed to a stop at the end of Nana's winding driveway, where two stone lions stood guard. Taking a deep breath of icy air, I climbed the bus steps and dropped into the green padded seat three rows behind the driver. My brother slid in beside me.

Thirty pairs of eyes bored into us.

"Who are they?" someone whispered.

"New kids. Fourth- and fifth-graders."

"From Iowa, I heard!"

I resisted the urge to sink down into the seat to escape the stares. Instead, I pulled off my red mittens and on the frosted window scratched a tic-tac-toe board. "Hey, Tyler, wanna play?"

"Nah." When he removed his hat, Tyler's brown hair sprang up like cornstalks after a windstorm—tilting every which way. He bent over his library book, *Secrets of the Solar System*. It smelled of glue and fresh ink. His glasses sat crookedly on his nose as he thumped his forefinger on a page. "Could be a parallel universe out there," he said. "Someday we could travel into another dimension of space and time."

Chrissa

"Changing schools is like entering a parallel universe," I said, staring out the window and thinking of my old school. Back home, I could walk to school with my friends instead of having to ride a bus. Although we'd moved only a few days ago, my old home seemed like a distant planet. On the drive north to Minnesota, Dad had tried to reassure me, "Before you know it, summer will be here and you can have Amanda come visit." But summer was light-years away.

I marked an X in the grid's upper left corner and then an O in the center, and then I rubbed it all away. I didn't want to play alone. I put my mittens back on and pressed them to my nose. The damp yarn reminded me of Cosmos and Checkers, Nana's new mini llamas. When I had met them a few days ago, I'd stood nervously outside of their stalls. "Do they bite?" I'd asked.

My grandma had laughed. "No, but if they're upset, they might spit. But only at each other—not at people."

Checkers is black and white, and Cosmos, who's going to have a baby this fall, is white all over. Nana had said that in a few months she would shear them and then wash, card, and spin the fleece into yarn. I would be around to help, now that we'd moved in with Nana.

Parallel Universe

As the bus hummed with chatter, a pinching emptiness filled my chest. I missed my old school and my friends Haley and Amanda. I missed Grandpa, too, and all his dumb jokes. Since he had died last fall, Nana's big house just hadn't been the same without him.

This morning Mom had poked her head into my room and said, "Time to get up, sleepyhead!" Mom is a doctor, just as Grandpa had been, and she was wearing her white medical coat over her regular clothes. She sat on the edge of my bed.

"Doctor Meg Maxwell?" I asked, tapping at her plastic name tag.

"Yes, Miss Chrissa Maxwell?" She smiled.

"Do you have a shot or a pill for new-school pain?"

Like a brown-feathered hen, she had pecked my forehead with a kiss. "There," she said. "Chrissa, I know you're a little scared, but you'll do just fine."

The bus driver slowed to a stop and cranked the doors open. "Here you go! Slowly now—no pushing!"

I paused outside the brick building, reading the name: Edgewater Elementary. Tyler was already heading through the doors. "C'mon, Chrissa," he called. He's only eleven months older than I am, but nothing seems to scare him. "You can't put it off forever. Time for liftoff!"

Chrissa

Red and pink hearts decorated the hallways. Next to my birthday, Valentine's Day is my favorite day of the whole year. It's actually tomorrow, but our new teachers had let us know that the school would be celebrating today, which is why Tyler and I were starting school on a Friday—Friday the thirteenth!

As Tyler headed off down the hall, I stepped through the doorway of Room 103. At the chalkboard, a man wearing a jacket, khaki pants, and loafers scribbled away. Then he twisted around, craning his head of thinning hair toward me.

"You must be Chrissa Maxwell! I'm Mr. Beck. Everyone's excited to have you here. Did you get the list I sent?"

I nodded. He'd sent a list of twenty-four names, including mine, so I would know everyone's names and how many valentines to bring. Since arriving at Nana's, I'd worked hard to make special ones for my new class-mates. Right now he pointed to a desk near the door. "In January, I let the class choose cluster partners," he explained. "There's one open seat in Cluster Four." Then he went back to writing on the board.

"Okay," I said, moving my things right in. I unpacked my button-decorated notebooks and organized my cloth-covered containers of markers, pencils, pens, and crayons. As other students arrived, I looked around, wondering who in this class might become a friend.

Three girls sauntered in and sat down at my cluster. I glanced up and smiled. "Hi," I said. "I'm Chrissa."

No response, but the girl with long dark-brown hair offered me a halfhearted smile.

As more students arrived, whispers fluttered around the room.

"Uh-oh."

"The new girl's stuck with the Queen Bees!"

"You mean the *Mean* Bees," someone else whispered. "*Bzzz!*"

This didn't sound good, but I remembered Nana's advice. *If you want a friend, be a friend. Don't wait for others to say hi. Just introduce yourself.* She has so many helpful tips, she should write her own book, *Just Ask Nana.*

I tried again. "Hi, I'm Chrissa Maxwell."

The three girls, who all wore ponytails, were busy talking to one another. Grandpa had always had a joke, so I tried humor. "Hey, is it Ponytail Day?"

They glanced my way but shifted their backs toward me. Since they weren't going to be friendly, I studied the names on their desks and tried to match them with their traits.

Tara. Long pale-blonde hair. Probably the prettiest girl in the class. And very petite. Tara. **T** for Tiny.

Jadyn. Round face, wavy hair, and intense green eyes. Jadyn. **J** for Jade-green eyes.

Sonali. Silky dark-brown hair and dark-brown eyes. Sonali. **S** for Silky hair.

And me. **Chrissa Marie Maxwell. C** for Curious about these unfriendly girls. **M** for Missing my old friends. And **M** for Missing my old school.

Lucky me. I'd just fallen into an unfriendly hive.

2

Valentine Troubles

After morning announcements, Mr. Beck introduced me and asked, "Chrissa, would you come to the front and tell us a little about yourself?"

I hesitated, feeling shy, but forced myself from my seat toward the board and faced the class. "Um, hi, I'm Chrissa. My brother, Tyler, is in Mrs. Ratworth's fifth-grade class. We just moved here from Iowa to live with Nana—my grandma—on Lake Chandler."

I wasn't sure what else to say.

I was relieved when a hand rose. "Why'd you move?" someone asked.

"Um, well, after my grandpa died last fall, Nana said the house was too big for her all alone. Plus, my mom was interested in working at a bigger hospital."

Mr. Beck asked, "Any more questions?"

A boy's hand shot straight up, even though he slouched so low in his seat, I thought he might slide to the floor.

"Joel?"

"So, did you live on a farm with tractors and combines and stuff like that?" His question made it sound like I'd lived on another planet.

I fidgeted with the ribbon on my dress. "No. We lived in town, but now, at Nana's, it's a little like a farm. She has two mini llamas."

From Cluster Four, Jadyn raised her hand. "I heard llamas spit, which would be, like, so gross?"

"Some do," I said, trying to remember what Nana had told me, "but it's usually at each other and only when they're mad. But they're really cute. Um, I guess that's all."

Everyone clapped politely. As I sat down, Tara whispered to Sonali and Jadyn, but loudly enough so that I could hear, "Rich kid. Everyone who lives on Lake Chandler is a snob." She flipped her ponytail over her shoulder and then tapped her polished nails on her desk.

I frowned. Snob? My grandpa hadn't been a snob, and Nana is the kindest person I know. Just because someone has a big house doesn't make her a bad person. I couldn't understand why these girls were being so mean. Before I had a chance to reply, Mr. Beck announced, "Class, please take out your math books."

I was actually happy to work on division. Anything to get my mind away from the rest of my cluster.

The day passed at the speed of a glacier. Several

kids smiled at me, but no one really took the time to talk to me. Near the day's end, Mr. Beck finally said, "Okay, now it's time to pass out your valentines." Along with the rest of the class, I jumped up from my seat.

"Oh, wait," Tara whispered, waving the rest of Cluster Four closer as she scribbled on the back of a heart-shaped piece of construction paper. "I totally forgot about one for Gwen!" Then she showed us. It read:

> *Roses are red,*
> *Violets are blue.*
> *You're the Loser Girl*
> *And no one likes you!*
> *Ha ha—just kidding!*
> *Happy Valentine's Day*
> *from Guess Who?*

The other girls all laughed and for a second, I giggled, too, feeling part of an inside joke. This must be a joke between Tara and this Gwen girl. At least I hoped so. Because if I got that card, *I* sure wouldn't like it.

Then we moved from desk to desk, tucking cards and candies into the "mailboxes" made from decorated paper milk or juice cartons. I thought it was nice of Mr. Beck to have put one on my desk, too. I navigated the desk clusters and mailboxes, delivering silver-wrapped chocolate kisses attached to hearts. I'd spent hours in Nana's sunroom cutting heart shapes from red and purple felt, and then gluing and stitching on pink lace, iridescent sequins, and buttons for decoration.

At one desk, a girl with sunny blonde hair and overgrown bangs sat hanging her head. Either she'd made it speedily around the room or she hadn't given out any valentines. Maybe she was part of a religious group that didn't celebrate holidays. I put a valentine in her mailbox anyway. When she glanced up with big brown eyes, she reminded me of a cute little mouse.

"Hi. Happy Valentine's Day," I said with a smile.

I was the last to sit back down, and I couldn't wait to see what was in my mailbox. I looked in.

It was *empty*, except for one card.

Heat rushed up my neck to my face. It didn't make any sense. I didn't expect to get tons of valentines, but only *one?* I thought everyone exchanged treats or cards with everybody. Mr. Beck had put my name on the valentine list—I'd seen it there. When I opened the one lonely envelope and pulled out the card, it was signed "G.T."

"Who's G.T.?" I whispered aloud.

Jadyn squeaked over my shoulder. "Oh, Gwen

Valentine Troubles

*My valentines mailbox was **empty**, except for one card.*

Thompson?" She pointed to the girl I had just noticed, who now was tucked into her shoulders like a cornered mouse.

"Ohhh," Tara said in a voice just quiet enough not to draw attention from Mr. Beck, who was on the other side of the room. "Gwen Thompson is the Loser Girl. Yeah, you two could have your own club. You certainly aren't in ours." Jadyn and Sonali cracked up.

I'd seen older girls like this before. On the playground, they whispered and giggled about others and on the bus they refused to give up saved seats. They treated other kids as if they were invisible—or worse, lowly as worms. I ached to be around my old friends instead of these girls. But I met Tara's eyes and spoke up. "Who says I want to be in your club anyway?"

Tara mimicked me with a toss of her head. *"Who says I want to be in your club anyway?"*

I groaned in frustration.

Just then, Mr. Beck turned toward us.

Tara's expression changed to mock hurt. "C'mon, Chrissa. Don't overreact. I'm just having a little fun."

"Yeah," Jadyn whispered. "She's just joking around? She didn't, like, mean anything by it?"

I didn't want to argue with them. Besides, it bugged me the way Jadyn turned every sentence into, *like, a question?* To avoid them, I glanced back inside my mailbox. That's when I noticed that the whole back had been cut into a big flap!

"Wait a second—the back of my mailbox opens up." I bent down to examine the floor between our clustered desks. No valentines had fallen there.

Tara popped her head under the desks, too. "Didn't get any valentines?" she whispered. "How sad!"

And then Sonali and Jadyn started giggling.

I sat up straight, too upset to speak. I didn't want to jump to any conclusions. It was possible that I had received only one valentine, but my gut told me they had been *stolen*.

3

Unexpected Call

Before I could say a word, Mr. Beck returned to the front of the room and sat on the edge of his desk. "Fourth grade, listen up! We have only a few more minutes. If anyone still needs to turn in registration forms for swimming, Monday's the deadline." He walked to my desk and handed me a form. "Chrissa, if you're interested in a two-week practice for Edgewater's Swim Club, you'll need to bring this back on Monday. It's fun—and I heard there's a really great coach."

Other students chuckled.

One boy shouted, "*You're* the coach!"

"Anyway, don't forget the form on Monday," Mr. Beck added. "Swimming starts that afternoon."

When the bell rang, Mr. Beck stood at the door, shaking hands with students as they poured out. I scanned the classroom. Maybe I could find a stash of valentines with my name on them. I stalled until I was the last one to leave, wondering if I should tell Mr. Beck—but then I'd be tattling and I figured that the mean Queen Bees might make things worse for me.

Mr. Beck shook my hand. "Chrissa, I hope you

had a good first day. Have a great weekend!"

"You, too," I said. Still I lingered. "Um, Mr. Beck, do you need help cleaning up after school today?" It would give me time to search.

He laughed. "Thanks, Chrissa, but not today. I'm surprising my wife with a day-before-Valentine's-Day date, so I'm heading out, too." He scooted me out the door as he turned the lights off. "Now don't miss your bus!"

I found a seat and Tyler soon settled in beside me, book in hand, as always. I was about to ask him if he'd gotten many valentines when two of the Mean Bees—Tara and Jadyn—hopped on the bus. My stomach turned like a corkscrew.

"Hi, Tyler!" Tara said, nearing our seat. "Heard you're new!" She smiled sweetly at him. She *was* pretty—on the outside.

He looked up from his book in surprise. "Uh, oh—hi."

Jadyn followed behind and smiled at Tyler, too. I'd just landed on Planet Weird. Why were they being so friendly to my brother?

He's smart about lots of things, but not about how things work with other kids. When they were beyond earshot, I whispered in his ear, "Tyler, don't trust them."

He flipped a page. "You're just jealous they said hi. Y'know, not everyone thinks I'm a geek."

I gazed outside and chewed on my lower lip. The bus rumbled along winding roads past houses, old and new, and pine, oak, and elm trees frosted white. Snowflakes fell against the windows and melted into tiny puddles.

As the bus dropped us off, Tara and Jadyn chorused, "Bye, Tyler!"

I rolled my eyes. They had to be doing it to bug me.

Three inches of fresh snow topped the two stone lions. With my mitten, I brushed off their stone ears, muzzles, and manes. "Tyler, remember how Grandpa said they protect everyone who passes through the gate?"

"'Guardians of the realm,'" Tyler added, waiting for me. "I miss Grandpa. It's not the same here without him."

"I know."

When I was little, I had imagined the lions coming to life at night to prowl around the rose hedges, the gazebo, and the shoreline to keep out intruders and keep everyone inside safe. I wished they could guard me at Edgewater Elementary now. They would sit on either side of me. Then, when the girls in my cluster made mean comments or stole from me, the lions would stare them down and roar. I knew it was just a stupid wish, but after only one day at Edgewater Elementary, I never wanted to return.

"Chrissa, what'd'ya think of the art teacher?" Tyler reached into a snowdrift and packed a snowball. "Did you have her today?"

The image of Ms. Rundell—with her purple glasses, hearty laugh, loosely pulled-back hair, and sparkly wand—made me smile. After she'd given us our assignment, she'd walked around with her wand and in an all-knowing voice had said things like, "You *will* create something marvelous!" and "True genius lies within *you!*" and to me she'd said, "I see *true talent,* Christina!" When the class laughed, she corrected herself. "I mean, Chrissa!"

"I have her fifth hour," I said. "She's really fun."

We kicked snow as we walked up the driveway. Grandpa's old John Deere tractor rumbled toward us like a green beetle with a lopsided antenna. As snow arched through the air from its shoot, Dad waved from the cab.

"He's like a little kid," Tyler said.

"Yeah, he loves that thing."

Chrissa

Tyler threw his snowball at the cab but missed. There is nothing Dad loves more than a good snowball fight, but today he just waved. We passed the small red barn and the three-stall garage on the left and the two-stall garage on the right. It had a new sign above the door that read MAXWELL POTTERY. Dad is a potter, and here at Nana's house he has a ton more studio space. Plus he gets to ride Grandpa's old tractor. No wonder *he* had wanted to move.

Climbing the steps to Nana's Victorian home is like stepping back in time. I love its gingerbread trim, its wraparound porch with the sloping green floor, white railings, and wicker furniture now covered in canvas for the winter. I've always loved visiting—but now it's supposed to be my home. *Weird.* Instead of a normal doorbell, the carved entry door has a brass knocker with a lion's head. I lifted it and knocked three times—*bang, bang, bang!*

Nana opened the door, and the aroma of freshly baked chocolate-chip cookies rolled out. "You two don't have to knock," she said. "You live here now, y'know." She was still in her fuchsia workout jacket and pants. Every afternoon she works out at the Edgewater Community Center, one block from school. But even with all that exercise, Nana still has a huggably soft body—unlike the thin and wiry instructors who teach the classes at the center. Nana tucked her bobbed gray hair behind her ears. Though her eyelids were rimmed red from crying, she smiled at us. "Hungry for cookies?"

"You bet!" Tyler said, dumping his backpack and jacket on the floor.

She turned. "Uh-uh." She pointed. "There's the closet."

Tyler groaned, but we promptly put away our boots, hats, mittens, and jackets and set our backpacks on the shelf.

When Nana went back into the kitchen, Tyler whispered, "She's like Central Command! We can't get away with anything."

"Yeah, she's tough," I agreed. "Even when she's feeling sad about Grandpa."

Things were a lot more casual at our old house, with everything thrown everywhere most of the time. But Nana had made it clear that keeping an orderly house was her one requirement of house sharing.

The sound of dripping came from the nearest bathroom. I waved Tyler over and we peeked in. Under a glow of stained-glass light, Nana's Siamese cat pawed at the water that trickled from the faucet. Nana usually allows Keefer a few minutes every day in the sink. He whines outside the bathroom door until someone turns on the water. Now he glanced at us with his slanted blue eyes, as if to ask, *What?*

"Keefer," Tyler laughed, "you are such a silly, goofy cat."

"At least he's a clean cat," I said.

"Then that makes him a silly, goofy, clean cat."

As we walked past the formal dining room, the hallway phone rang.

"Nana, should I get it?" I asked, fingers crossed that it was Amanda.

"You live here, remember?" Nana called back sweetly. "Just answer it."

I picked up the receiver. Nana insists on keeping her old black rotary dial phone. No call-waiting. No caller ID. It's ancient. "Hello?" I said.

"Chrissa?"

I didn't answer. I thought I recognized the voice of one of the Mean Bees, but I wasn't sure which one. It wasn't the meanest one, but I couldn't believe they were bold enough to harass me at home, too! I made up my mind right then and there—I was *not* going back to Edgewater Elementary.

4

A Bad Joke

"Chrissa Maxwell?" the girl pressed. "Do I have the right number?"

"Yes," I said, wavering between hanging up and wanting to find out why I was getting a phone call.

"This is Sonali . . . Sonali Matthews, from Mr. Beck's class. Can you talk?"

Let's see, I thought. *Shall we talk about how three girls ruined my first day of school? How, because of them, I am not going back?*

I let the silence grow.

"Chrissa?"

"What?" I replied without a speck of enthusiasm. I pictured Sonali with her long silky hair, as slippery as her heart must be.

"I have to say I'm sorry. Plus, I have something for you. Can I stop by?"

I knew what Nana would say. *When someone says she's sorry, you need to forgive her.* My lips were glued together. The words just weren't there. "Now? Is this some kind of bad joke?"

"Yes. I mean, no—it's not a joke. And yes, I have

something. So *can* I come over? Right now?"

"Um, okay," I finally responded. I set down the phone and stared into the mirror above the small table.

"Chrissa? Coming for cookies?" Nana called.

"Just a minute, Nana." I stopped chewing my lower lip, combed my fingers through my hair, and then ran up the staircase to the third room on the left. My room. If Sonali was coming over, she might want to see my room.

Moving like a tornado, I tossed dirty socks and jeans into the laundry basket, rearranged my stuffed animals, and put my favorite—a buttery soft long-eared rabbit that I call Mopsy—on the center of my pillow. Then I straightened the circular sheers that hung over my bed and stood back. I'd worked magic—almost as if I'd waved Ms. Rundell's sparkly wand. *Phew!*

Not bad.

Hungry for cookies, I raced down the stairs. Just as my feet hit the landing, the knocker sounded. *Bang, bang!*

"I'll get it!" I called out.

I opened the door.

"Hi," Sonali said, holding a big red gift bag. I could tell the bag had been used before, which was cool. We recycle, too.

A Bad Joke

"Come in," I said, holding the door open. I wasn't sure, but Sonali almost looked as if she had been crying.

Standing behind her on the steps was Sonali's mother. "Go on now. You know why you're here. I'll wait in the car." She adjusted the bright silk shawl over her coat and then turned back toward a black Jetta, its tailpipe puffing white.

Sonali nodded and then stepped inside.

Suddenly I had the feeling that Sonali was being *made* to come over. *Made* to apologize. My mood dropped to my toes.

"Here," she said, handing me the bag. "These are your valentines. The ones that we—I mean *I*—took from your mailbox. Sorry."

A lump lodged itself in my throat.

I peered into the bag and saw a bunch of envelopes with my name on them. So the class *had* been prepared for my being there after all. I hadn't been left out. I felt a tiny bit better.

Sonali shifted her weight from one boot to another, as if waiting for something from me. Forgiveness, probably. But I wasn't ready to give her that, especially since she didn't really seem sorry. Or at least not sorry for what she'd done to me. If anything,

I guessed that she was sorry she'd gotten caught.

"Your mom's waiting," I said.

"Yeah, I better go."

The lump shifted just enough for me to ask, "But why did you do it?"

"Tara told me to."

"You do whatever she tells you?"

She looked beyond me to the grandfather clock in the hall. When she finally met my eyes, she answered. "She said to take them home and not say a word. But my mom found them. And, well, like I said . . . sorry."

My irritation flared. "So your mom made you return them. Did she make you say you're sorry?"

She nodded. "If it makes you feel any better, I'm grounded for the weekend. But my mom has to show a house right now, so I gotta go." She spun and pulled the door open, as if she couldn't wait to get away. She ran down the porch steps, through the falling snow, and hopped into the car, looking straight ahead. The car left tracks in the fresh snow as it pulled away.

I had hoped her visit would make me feel better, but now, holding my bag of valentines, I felt even worse.

By the time I entered the kitchen, Tyler was outside, piling up snowballs by the leafless willows. Nana was at the table, her teacup nesting in her hands.

A Bad Joke

"Who was that at the door, Chrissa?"

"Oh, a girl from my class. I, uh, forgot my valentines at school." I emptied the red bag onto the table.

The scent of Nana's peppermint tea teased my nose. "Why, that was awfully nice of her to bring them," she said and took a sip.

I let out an exaggerated sigh. "Yeah."

"Chrissa," she said, reaching for my hand. "What's wrong?"

If I were to tell her about my day, I'd probably start blubbering. How could I tell her it had been the worst day of my life? She'd feel awful for asking us to move in with her. I bit into the flesh of my lower lip. Besides, Nana had her own sadness with Grandpa gone. In comparison, what was a lousy day at a new school? "Nothing," I lied. "I guess I'm just missing Amanda and my old friends."

Her face softened with a faraway look. "Hmm. I know what you mean."

For a few moments, Nana and I gazed out the window, watching Tyler. Snowflakes continued to fall from the gray sky, turning the willow branches into a lacy tent of white. On the frozen lake, the rink we'd shoveled earlier had disappeared. If Amanda lived nearby, I would invite her to come over and help me

Chrissa

shovel—and then we'd skate together.

"Chrissa, why don't you give your friend a call?"

I jumped up. I hadn't seen Amanda in six days, but it seemed like six years. "Thanks, Nana!"

I ran to the hallway phone and dialed.

"Oh, Chrissa, I'm sorry," her mom said. "Amanda went with Haley's family for a Valentine's weekend in Des Moines. They're going to stay at a hotel and do some swimming and shopping. She'll be glad to hear you called. She really misses you, you know."

I hung up and gulped down my feelings. Then I trudged up the staircase to my bedroom for a good cry.

5

Llamas and Girls

Before I went to bed that night, Nana said, "How about going out to breakfast tomorrow morning, just you and me—and Cosmos and Checkers?"

I wasn't sure what llamas had to do with getting breakfast, but I didn't protest.

Early Saturday morning, as I followed Nana down the shoveled path to the small barn, I came up with a plan for never returning to Mr. Beck's class. I would be home-schooled, just like my cousins in Texas. Dad and Nana would be my teachers. All I had to do was talk them into it.

As we entered the barn, the llamas stood tall and curious in their stalls, their necks extended and ears alert. But with their long eyelashes, they seemed almost human.

"Hi, Cosmos! Hi, Checkers!" Nana called.

This time, I didn't flinch or back away. Instead, I stepped into Cosmos's stall and gave her a hug. Though llamas aren't big cuddlers, she gave me llama kisses—wobbly, warm, and harmless nibbles on my face. Unlike horses, llamas can't bite. They're more like cows that way, only a whole lot cuter.

Nana and I clipped on their lead ropes, tied them outside their stalls, and brushed their coats. Then we fed them grain from buckets. When Checkers finished her grain, she stretched her neck toward Cosmos to try to snitch from her bucket. Instantly, Cosmos flattened her ears and pressed her chest out in warning.

"Watch out, Nana!" I said. "Cosmos looks like she might kick!"

Nana moved aside and tugged on Checkers's lead rope. "Mind your own business, Checkers," she scolded. Then to me, she explained, "Llamas have a pecking order among themselves—so they sometimes fight over food and spit or kick sideways to show who's boss and to get their way. These two have accepted us as their leaders. Still, they act up with each other at times to show dominance."

"Just like with the Mean Bees," I said.

"Is that a TV show, or some music group?"

I laughed. "No, Nana. Just some girls at school."

With the Mean Bees, it seems like Tara shows dominance and Jadyn backs up whatever Tara says. And then Sonali *does* whatever Tara says—even if it means being mean to or hurting another girl. But girls aren't llamas. We're supposed to care about one another—at least that's what I've been taught. I shouldn't have to put up with being bossed around by other girls. But not being a llama, I can't just give a swift kick every time they bug me.

While Checkers waited, Cosmos finished her last bits of grain. Then we led them out to the van. Cosmos's white coat blended in with the fresh snow as she walked eagerly alongside me. She is pregnant, but she really doesn't look much wider yet than Checkers, who stopped every few feet to paw in the snow for a mouthful of frozen grass. Nana tugged Checkers forward. "C'mon, you little food hound."

I eyed the van, with its back doors open and the middle and back seats removed. I didn't know what Nana had in mind.

"In you go," Nana said to Cosmos. Apparently Cosmos loves van rides, because she hopped right in and then *kushed* by tucking her four legs under her body while holding her head upright. Head high, she peered out the side window.

Checkers danced back and forth, but Nana tapped her on the rump and finally she too hopped into the van and kushed. Then Nana closed the back doors. "Y'know, Chrissa, before Grandpa became too ill, we used to have full-sized llamas. Remember?"

Chrissa

I remembered being afraid of them, but I was smaller then and they were twice as big as Cosmos and Checkers.

"I remember," I said.

We climbed into the front seats.

"Grandpa and I used to take them to the nursing home on pet days to cheer people up. They could put a smile on the grumpiest of faces."

I twisted in my seat and scratched Cosmos. Her hair was so thick I could lose my hand in her coat. Nana was right—I found myself smiling at Cosmos's long lashes and sweet eyes.

As we drove past the stone lions and down the road, I wondered where Nana was heading. We wound past houses and then toward stores and gas stations, finally pulling in at a fast-food restaurant. "Here we are," Nana said.

She drove up to the speaker phone. "Good morning. We'd like two egg-and-sausage biscuits, two orange juices, one coffee, and one hot chocolate." Then we pulled forward to pick up our order. When the service window opened, Nana rolled down the car windows and Checkers craned her head out, too, like a fuzzy antenna—right behind Nana's.

The woman at the window shrieked. "What *is*

that thing?!" she asked Nana.

"A mini llama," Nana said calmly. "And her name is Checkers."

"Well, you scared me half to death!" Then the woman started laughing and called her coworkers to come and look. Pretty soon half a dozen workers were looking out the window at Checkers. Cosmos edged up between the seats, too, as if not to miss out on the fun.

"Oh, they're becoming regulars," one woman said. "They came through last week."

"They're adorable!" exclaimed another.

A car honked behind us.

"Guess we better go!" Nana said and waved good-bye. Just then two girls walked out of the restaurant and stepped in front of our van.

Nana braked.

My stomach lurched.

I couldn't believe it! What were the chances that two Mean Bees—Tara and Jadyn—would cross my path? *Please, please don't look at the van!* But Jadyn turned with a sleepy glance our way, and then she shrieked and pointed.

The car behind us honked again.

"Nana, go!" I pleaded.

"I can't run them over, Chrissa!"

Checkers pulled her head away from Nana's side and brought it alongside Cosmos's and my own. I must have looked like some weird three-headed creature. As the Bees scooted out of our path, they pointed and laughed.

To my dismay, Nana pulled into a parking space. "Time for breakfast!" she chirped.

I wanted to disappear. I'd never hear the end of this. I stared at the building across from the parking lot.

A knock came at Nana's window, and I forced myself to look.

Nana lowered the window. "Hi, girls," she said cheerily.

"Do those things poop in your van?" Tara asked.

Nana just laughed. "Not at all." To my horror, she reached down and picked up a coffee can. "Tell them, Chrissa." My tongue was stuck to the roof of my mouth. I shook my head mutely.

Nana shook the can. "No, they won't go in the van. But when we travel, I always bring along some 'llama beans' to sprinkle on the ground when we stop, so they'll know where to go. They're well-trained."

Jadyn wrinkled her nose at the can. "That's, like, disgusting?"

"They're just droppings," Nana said, giving the can another shake as proof.

The girls walked away, giggling.

Nana handed me a wrapped biscuit. "Here you go, dearie."

But I couldn't eat a thing.

When we returned to Nana's, Tyler dashed outside, yanking on his jacket. "Hey! Why didn't you two take me along with you?"

"You were sound asleep, Tyler," Nana said, "and Chrissa and I needed some girl time."

Then Tyler and I led Cosmos and Checkers around the snowy yard, and even into the gazebo. The llamas turned their banana-shaped ears toward every sound. When a neighbor's black Lab trotted over to investigate and sniffed too close to Cosmos, she lifted her hind leg in warning. Lucky for the dog, he got the message and kept his distance.

"See that?" I said to Tyler. "Cosmos just warned him. It's the same as my warning you about those girls on the bus. You think they're being friendly, but I mean it—they're *not* nice."

"Don't start." He held his hand out as if he were controlling traffic—the same signal Mom gives us when we start begging for something. If he wouldn't listen, how could I explain that their friendliness was the opposite of what it seemed? That they were acting nice only to get at me. It was a very turned-around kind of meanness.

After we'd wandered along the edge of the frozen bay a bit longer, we put the llamas away and headed inside.

Mom greeted me in the kitchen with a hug.

"There's my girl!" She always sleeps late on Saturdays, when she can, to catch up from her long workdays. When she goes to see her patients at the hospital or clinic, she always dresses up. But on Saturdays, she relaxes in jeans. Today her hair was in a ponytail.

I winced, remembering the Mean Bees. I suppose I could go to school on Monday with a ponytail to try to fit in with them, but then what? They'd change to headbands or something, just to be mean.

"What?" Mom asked. "Do I have something on my face?"

"No—it's just the ponytail. It reminds me of some girls at school, that's all."

"Not girls who are making you smile, I see. Tell me."

"Oh, I sit with three girls who wish I wasn't there." I wished that I could stop time and curl up in a soft chair with Mom and tell her all about the Bees. I wanted to tell her about everything, but I didn't want her to worry—and I didn't want to be a tattletale.

Mom spun me gently toward the table, where Nana, Dad, and Tyler were sitting. "It takes time to adjust to anything new," Mom said. "They'll come around. Just give it time, Chrissa."

Just time? Now I felt myself getting annoyed.

Chrissa

I sort of expected Nana not to get what I was going through, but I thought that Mom would see. *Why doesn't she get it? She was my age once. Didn't she know any mean girls then?* Giving it more time wasn't going to change a thing. I had a better idea—never go back. And right now was the perfect time to tell them about home-schooling.

Saturday's regular lunch was set out on the table: sloppy Joes, pickles, chips, and veggies and dip. It's the extent of Mom's cooking. Dad usually does most of the cooking, both because he likes to and because he's home more. Now he and Nana are sharing the cooking, just like they'd share in home-schooling me—at least when Dad wasn't too busy in his studio.

But before I could bring up my plan, Dad set his glass of milk down and said, "Hey, gang, I need your help. I'm in over my head. Last summer, Grandpa asked me to help with a fund-raiser by making two hundred bowls. I said yes. But that was before I knew we'd be moving. Somehow the delivery date crept up on me, and, well, frankly, I need some help."

"I'll help," Nana said.

"Thanks, Louise," he said with a wink. "I can always count on you."

Tyler screwed up his face. "My bowls aren't very good, Dad. They're more lopsided than round—more like comets than planets, if you get my point."

"Point taken," Dad replied. "But throwing the bowls isn't where I'm behind. I've already thrown and done the first firing of more than half of them. It's the glazing that's really got me in a pickle." He lifted a pickle from his plate to underscore his point. "If I didn't have that restaurant order to ship to Vermont in three weeks . . ."

Tyler piped up. "Hey, I know! You could ask our art teacher, Ms. Rundell. She's really nice, and if you tell her it's for a good cause, I bet she'd ask her classes to help."

Dad's brow relaxed and a smile crept over his face. "Perfecto! I'll talk to her first thing Monday."

"Great," I said under my breath. Now I'd have to return to Edgewater Awful Elementary, at least until Dad finished his project.

On Sunday the temperature dropped to ten degrees below zero and the wind flung bare willow branches like toothpicks across Nana's yard. I sat in the shelter of the sunroom with Nana, the fire in the big fieldstone fireplace warming us. Keefer curled himself into a ball at my feet and licked the toes of my socks.

"Keefer's a good foot warmer," I said, working at the craft table Nana had cleared for me to use.

"He's always liked you," said Nana.

I wished others liked me as much.

To cheer up my bedroom—and myself—I was decorating a throw pillow for my bed with sequins and shiny ribbons. While I cut and stitched, Nana was turning a basket of clean and carded llama fleece she'd bought from the llama raiser into yarn on her spinning wheel. It is amazing how something so clumpy can be reshaped into yarn and eventually into scarves, mittens, hats, and sweaters. If only I could reshape my life into something different.

"I know you're feeling blue about moving," Nana said.

I was startled by how well Nana read me. I guess she saw more than I'd thought. "It's that obvious?"

"Obvious, but not hopeless," she replied. She stopped her work and looked me in the eye. "Sometimes it helps to look for someone who could use a friend."

The lump in my throat that I'd kept pushing down all weekend nudged up again. And to make myself feel worse, I pictured Amanda with Haley in Des Moines, a trip Amanda and I had made once with *my* family. I could barely reply. Finally I whispered, "But I'm the one who needs a friend."

"Yes, I realize that." Nana reached over and drew a light line with her finger down the side of my cheek. "Still, it's something to think about."

The image of Gwen Thompson floated up in my mind. Gwen Thompson with the over-grown bangs. The one the Mean Bees called the "Loser Girl." Tara's words taunted me: *You two could start your own club.*

I wasn't sure Gwen was the kind of friend I had in mind. She was awfully quiet. And she seemed so *alone*. But then, it occurred to me that nothing would bug the Mean Bees more than if I befriended her. They'd rather see her lonely and friendless—someone they could tease. Like me. What if we teamed up? Maybe it was wrong to want to get back at the Bees that way. But Nana had said to look for someone who could use a friend.

And in Room 103, Gwen Thompson certainly wasn't winning a Miss Popularity contest.

6

Monday Mess

As my brother and I plopped into our bus seats on Monday morning, Tara and Jadyn called out, "Hi, Tyler!" I braced myself for teasing about "llama beans," but to my relief, they didn't say anything more as the bus bounced along. Maybe Mom was right. Maybe giving it time would change things.

Gazing out my window, I thought about my newest plan to become friends with Gwen Thompson—*if* Gwen wanted to be friends. There's power in numbers, isn't there?

But the only thing I honestly looked forward to, the only shimmering bright spot at the end of my school day, was *swimming*. Tyler and I had gotten our registration forms signed by Dad before leaving the house, because Mr. Beck had made it clear: no registration form—no swimming. I was all set.

I breathed against the frosted pane, melted a tiny round circle, and gazed out. The sun glinted high in a watery blue sky and I imagined it was a huge upside-down lake, like Lake Chandler in reverse. The summer when I was five, Grandpa taught me to swim in the lake. I had talked so much about being a mermaid that Nana had made me a shimmery green swimming outfit with an elastic waist and fringe around the ankles. Every time I wore it over my swimsuit and fins, I *became* a mermaid. My eyes grew so red from trying to see underwater that Nana bought me a mask and snorkel, too. Clams and crayfish became octopuses and giant squid. Sand castles turned into royal palaces. I had tried to get Tyler to join in, but he'd been more interested in launching Lego astronauts from the dock than in playing mermaids with me.

The bus stopped, jolting me out of my daydream. Reluctantly, I shouldered my backpack, headed into school, and trudged to Room 103.

When I approached my desk, Tara pinched her nose. "Whoa! Something stinks."

Jadyn clamped her nose with her thumb and forefinger. "P.U.!"

"Hey, today's taco day, Chrissa. Are you going to have some *llama beans* with your taco?" Tara asked.

Though Sonali hadn't seen the llamas, she pinched her nose, too.

I set my backpack beside my desk, sat down, and lifted my desktop, pretending to organize my boxes. This was going to be another awful day.

Luckily, Mr. Beck kept the class jumping all morning from one subject to the next. Before I knew it, I was in line for lunch, right behind Gwen. The smell of seasoned taco filling wafted through the cafeteria. I remember Nana saying, *People love to talk about themselves, so just ask.* So when I picked up my plastic tray, I asked, "Gwen, are you going to swim practice?"

She nearly jumped at hearing her name. "Uh-huh," she said so quietly that I strained to hear. "I'm sort of scared, though. I don't really know how to swim."

I was stunned that someone in fourth grade wouldn't know how to swim, but then I'd had the chance to spend a few weeks every summer at Lake Chandler—plus back home I went swimming as often as I could. "You'll learn fast. And if you need help with anything, just ask. I could help."

She glanced up from under her bangs. "Thanks."

Someone snickered and I looked back over my shoulder. The Mean Bees were behind us by a few people and Tara rolled her eyes at me. I pretended I didn't care.

Monday Mess

In art class, I was surprised to see Dad standing next to Ms. Rundell. He winked at me when he saw me walk in. I gave him a small wave as I took my seat at one of the large black tables with wooden stools—right beside Gwen. So far, my plan to become friends was working out perfectly.

"Hi again," I said.

She tilted her head and peered sideways with her wide brown eyes. "Hi," she whispered. She didn't exactly smile, but it was better than nothing at all.

"Class," Ms. Rundell began. "We have a professional potter—Paul Maxwell, who is also Chrissa's father—here with us today. The fourth- and fifth-grade teachers and I met with him this morning to hear his proposal, and, well, I can't wait to tell you about it. As part of our art class, you will each paint a bowl that Mr. Maxwell has thrown on his wheel. You'll be free to design and glaze the bowl as you like, but there's one catch."

The room quieted.

"You must be willing to give it away."

"Give it away?" someone repeated.

"In a couple of weeks," Ms. Rundell continued, "there's a fund-raiser for Sunrise House at the Community Center. People who attend will be served homemade soup in beautiful bowls—and as a thank-you for coming and for their financial donations, they get to keep their bowls."

"Dirty bowls?" someone asked. "That would be pretty gross."

"Oh, don't worry," Ms. Rundell replied. "I'm sure bowls will be washed before donors take them home. Yes, Joel?"

"What's Sunrise House?" It was the boy who had asked if I lived on a farm.

Ms. Rundell looked from Joel to my dad.

"It's a nearby house—" Dad explained, "—an old mansion, really—that offers a safe shelter for women and children in need of housing."

Ms. Rundell picked up her wand and swirled it above us. "If you think this is a marvelous idea, raise your hand!"

Every hand in the room flew up, except for Gwen's, which she lifted with little enthusiasm only a few inches off the table. Maybe she didn't like the idea of parting with something she made, which I could understand. Anytime I make something and give it away—like the scarf I knitted for Amanda last Christmas—it always pains me a little. But Nana always says, *A gift worth wanting is a gift worth giving.*

Ms. Rundell continued, "The classroom work is required, but the rest of this is a volunteer opportunity. My hope is that each and every one of you will help with decorating, serving, and yes, even cleaning up at the supper." My dad tapped her shoulder and whispered in her ear. "Oh, and one more thing. Mr. Maxwell has invited us all over to see his studio on Saturday morning and help out with more bowls, if you'd like. I'll give you more details later, but for now, start thinking about how you'll decorate your bowl."

My classmates might come over? This was news to me. *Why hadn't he told me this? What if the Mean Bees come over?* As Dad left, I wished I could leave with him and never return.

After art, we headed back across the hall to our homeroom. Before I sat down, Mr. Beck waved a large manila envelope in my direction. "Chrissa, would you please run this to the office?"

"Sure," I said, happy to put off sitting with my cluster, if only for a few more minutes.

"Already his favorite," Tara whispered.

I ignored her comment and walked up to his desk, but the Bees followed at my heels, abuzz with comments.

"Can I do it?" Jadyn whined. "She's new, and like,

Chrissa

I've never been asked to take something to the office?"

Sonali added with a toss of her hair, "I'll do it!"

Something sharp poked into the small of my back. It hurt, but I didn't flinch, not wanting to make a scene. I clenched my jaw and focused on Mr. Beck.

"*Chrissa*, please take it directly to the office. It's all the registration forms for swimming, due there in exactly—" he glanced at the clock above the door, "—three minutes. Now, I believe I called *Chrissa*, not Cluster Number Four. Take your seats, girls."

I was glad to get out of there. As I headed down the hallway, I heard Mr. Beck announce, "I've been reminded that we didn't take a restroom break last hour. So go now if you need to." A rush of footsteps and chatter followed.

Before going into the office, I hurried into the girls' restroom. I had to know what the Mean Bees had done to my shirt. In the bathroom stall, I set the packet on the floor and then craned my neck to look at the small of my back. When that didn't work, I yanked off my shirt to examine it. I squinted at the back of my shirt, and sure enough, there was a tiny pencil-point-sized hole. I touched the small of my back, winced, and pulled out a small piece of lead from a mechanical pencil. I huffed, "Great."

Monday Mess

Voices filled the bathroom as stall doors opened and closed. I double-checked that my door was locked. I didn't want to be embarrassed by someone swinging it open and finding me with my shirt off. That was the last thing I needed.

Swoosh! A soft scrape across the floor of my stall made my stomach drop. I glanced down to see the edge of the packet disappear into the stall on my left.

"Hey, what's this?" came Tara's voice, followed by a chorus of giggles. "Wasn't this supposed to go directly to the office?"

A nearby toilet flushed with a roaring *swoosh.*

"No! You wouldn't!" I yanked my shirt back on as fast as my fingers could fumble, but it seemed to take me forever.

When I finally stormed out, the bathroom was nearly empty. The only other girl left was Gwen, who was washing her face at the sink.

"Where did they go?" I asked.

Her bangs and eyelashes were damp, making her eyes look even bigger. She shrugged her shoulders.

I stepped into the hallway, uncertain if I should return to the classroom and tell Mr. Beck exactly what had happened. I turned this way, then that, circling slowly. They wouldn't really have flushed all the registration forms, would they?

If I were to tell Mr. Beck the truth, he'd know I had disobeyed his order to go straight to the office. *And* I would be tattling, wouldn't I?

I had enough troubles stacking up against me without adding *tattler* to the top of the heap.

Then I saw Tara come out of the principal's office. At least that meant she'd probably turned in the envelope, so maybe I didn't need to say anything to Mr. Beck about it. I let out my breath, which I hadn't realized that I'd been holding.

As I stepped back into our classroom, Sonali and Jadyn were chatting about practice and what kind of ranking they hoped to get on the team. They ignored me and acted as if nothing had happened.

I sat down, but my heart thudded in my ears.

Seconds later, Tara stepped in and took her seat. She was absolutely glowing.

"Don't worry, Chrissa," she whispered smugly. "I'm not a tattletale, so Mr. Beck won't ever have to know how irresponsible you were with that envelope. Imagine just leaving it lying on the bathroom floor! How *could* you?"

7

Bzzz

After school, I met up with Tyler. Together we followed the shoveled sidewalk from Edgewater Elementary to the Community Center for swim practice.

"Hey, Tyler and Chrissa!" Sonali called from up ahead. She was alone for once, and she waited as we approached. Then she smiled at us.

I didn't smile back.

She fell into step with us, with Tyler in the middle. "So, you're both going to swim club practice?"

"You bet," Tyler answered. "Can't wait!" He pulled his steamed-up glasses off and tucked them into his jacket pocket. Glancing sideways at him, I had to admit that he was getting cuter as he got older. The thought crossed my mind that maybe the kids at Edgewater saw him differently than I did. Maybe I had it wrong about the Mean Bees and their friendliness toward him.

"I'm really interested in diving," Tyler said.

"Me, too," Sonali replied, "but Tara's the one who's really good. She's the best girl diver in fourth grade."

I slowed my pace so that I fell a few steps behind Tyler and Sonali. I just couldn't trust her or any of the Bees. I flashed on the manila packet disappearing into the nearby stall. Everything had happened so fast. Tara had returned to our classroom with that smug expression, and before I knew it, school was dismissed. I hoped against hope that Tara really *had* turned the envelope in, even though she had played another mean trick on me. My jacket was warm, but I shuddered.

"Sonali," I ventured, "um, do you know what happened to that packet?"

She shook her head and her glossy hair *swooshed* from beneath her hat. "I have an idea, but I'm, well, I'm not sure." And then she darted ahead and joined Tara and Jadyn, who were waiting inside the glass doors of the center.

Tyler and I pushed through the doors and humid, chlorine-scented air engulfed us. The woman behind the registration counter pointed us toward the locker rooms.

"Last one in's a hard-boiled egg," Tyler said, turning right toward the boys' locker room.

"You mean a *rotten* egg," I called back.

"Whatever!"

As I entered the girls' locker room, Tara's voice

Bzzz

snagged me like a fish on a hook.

"—can't wait to see Chrissa's face. It's going to be so funny!" Jadyn and Sonali laughed, and then Tara said, "*Shhh.* She might be coming."

I pretended not to hear and went to the farthest set of yellow lockers. Their voices were lost in the clang of slamming metal doors and the hum of muffled chatter. A few mothers were there with younger girls. "Hurry up, honey," one mom said. "You don't want to be late for your first practice."

I peeled off so many layers—mittens, hat, jacket, boots—you'd think I lived in Antarctica. In the past, when I had visited the center with Nana and Grandpa, I had loved the buzzing voices of families, the cheery yellow and orange locker room, the blue stripes marking swimming lanes, and the resounding *thud* of the diving board. But now my stomach churned. Even though I love to swim and had been excited about the swim club and tryouts, I should never have signed up. I hadn't even entered the pool and already the Mean Bees had ruined everything.

To avoid them, I dawdled, changing into my swimsuit slowly, until the locker room was empty, quiet enough to hear my own breathing.

I closed my locker softly, walked past the empty

shower area—expecting trouble at any moment—and slipped through the door labeled "POOL."

Kids of various ages were clustered around high-school-age instructors. A few parents sat on the bleachers. I found Tyler with a group of kids who looked like ten- and eleven-year-olds. At its center, the Mean Bees hovered near the instructor, a girl with pigtails and pink lip gloss who was studying papers on her clipboard.

"What took you so long?" Tyler whispered. "Our instructor, Liz, already took roll call."

"Did she call my name?"

He shook his head.

Just then, Mr. Beck, wearing athletic pants, flip-flops, and a T-shirt, gathered everyone at the bleachers. "Welcome, swimmers and divers!" He explained how the next two weeks would allow us to improve our skills, regardless of our ability level. We would work with high-school students who knew all about competitive swimming and diving. Finally, he smiled and said, "And I want you to have fun! That's an order."

When we gathered back into our groups, I raised my hand, but Liz didn't seem to see me. "Excuse me?" I called out. "Am I in this group?"

"What's your name?"

"Chrissa Maxwell. I'm ten."

Liz ran her finger down a sheet on her board, mashed her glossy lips together, and then shook her head. "No, you're not on this list. Did you turn in a form?"

"Yes."

She pointed to the bleachers. "Talk to Mr. Beck, but he'll probably make you wait until the paperwork is in. If so, sit near Lane One, so that you can watch, and then remember to bring the form tomorrow. Sorry."

Tara nearly doubled over with silent laughter and both Jadyn and Sonali pressed their hands to their mouths. I glared at them and then turned away, piecing the prank together as I padded barefoot to the bleachers. The packet had been turned in at the office with one form missing. *Mine.*

I'd never really hated anyone before, but a hot ember was beginning to burn in my chest.

Fuming, I watched as the members of my group demonstrated their breaststroke skills. "Remember to extend your arms and legs fully with each stroke!" Liz called out, walking along the swim lane.

When Gwen jumped in, she did a dog paddle but her feet kept sinking to the bottom. She couldn't even float! "Gwen," Liz said, "hop out. I'm sending you to work with the eight- and nine-year-olds to catch up."

Tara and Jadyn smirked as Gwen climbed out and headed to the opposite side of the pool. I felt bad for her, but I could see that she definitely needed more practice on the basics.

I rarely use the cell phone that Tyler and I share for emergencies, but my situation qualified. I jumped up, hurried back to the locker room, and grabbed the phone from my backpack. "Dad," I blurted, "I lost my registration form . . . I don't know what happened to it, Dad, it just got lost . . . Can you hurry?" Not telling him the truth made my stomach hurt more. But I knew that if I told him the real story, he'd make me rat the Bees out.

As I waited again on the bleachers, I stared at Tara and Jadyn and Sonali—letting them know that I wasn't laughing. But I wasn't crying, either. I was angry. For an instant I wished that my dad were a high-powered attorney instead of a potter. I'd have him sue the Mean Bees for every last penny in their piggy banks. I knew it was a ridiculous idea, but the notion made me feel a little better. It was better than just feeling frustrated. And powerless. And even a little bit scared.

Instead, I just waited and watched. Time dragged by and Dad didn't show up as quickly as I'd hoped.

Bzzz

The Red Group, as my level was called, took turns swimming in Lane One while Liz observed their backstroke, sidestroke, and crawl.

When a bell rang, Mr. Beck called out, "Fifteen minutes of free swim!" I watched and chewed on the edges of my fingernails.

Minutes passed before I noticed the Bees and some other girls near the deep end, playing catch with a ball. Gwen stood nearby in shoulder-deep water.

"Hey, Gwen!" someone called, tossing the ball toward her.

Gwen caught it in both hands, almost smiled, and sent it flying toward another girl, but the ball was too high.

Tara jumped into the air, caught the ball, then twisted backward and went under. She popped up and held it high. "Got it!" Then she threw the ball to Sonali, who threw it to Jadyn, who threw it back to Gwen again. I was surprised. I hadn't expected the Bees to stoop to playing ball with someone they called the Loser Girl. Something was up.

Gwen bounced up and down, the water rising to her neck as she bobbed closer to the deep end. I watched her closely, knowing that she wasn't a good swimmer and thinking she should stay where it was shallower to be safe. But with each ball toss, she inched deeper.

"This one's for you, Gwen!" Tara called out. She sent the ball flying close to Gwen but just over her head. Gwen jumped up and almost caught the ball, but then twisted in the direction of the deep end and slipped under.

"Oh, no!" I said, jumping up from the bleacher.

I waited for her to come back up, figuring Tara would have an insult ready. But Gwen didn't surface. I glanced over at Liz and the other instructors. Wasn't someone watching? I ran—even though the number one rule in the pool is No Running.

A whistle, shrill and clear, blew.

"Someone's under!" I called. I grabbed the life ring from the wall and swung it out into the deep end where Gwen had gone under. At the same moment, Mr. Beck jumped in fully clothed, swam down, and surfaced with Gwen in a lifesaving grip, pulling her to the edge. He rolled her onto the cement and then climbed up beside her.

Immediately, Gwen coughed and hacked up water, and it seemed that everyone in the pool had suddenly gathered around. "You're gonna be okay, Gwen," said Mr. Beck. "You just took in a little water.

Good thinking, there, Chrissa," he said to me.

When Gwen sat up, someone draped a towel around her shoulders. After she stopped coughing, she started to cry. Soon students and instructors filtered away. Mr. Beck left when he was sure she was okay.

The Mean Bees hovered around us.

"I didn't mean to throw the ball into the deep end," Tara said, almost sincerely.

I turned and looked up at her. "You meant it! I was watching!"

"How can you say that?" Tara said. "I wouldn't—"

"The ball just went a little too far," Jadyn chimed in. "We were just, like, playing catch?"

I noticed that Sonali hadn't said a word. She snugged her arms across her chest, shivering. When she glanced my way, a cloud of uncertainty crossed her brow. I couldn't figure her out. Sometimes she seemed nice, but then just as quickly she fell right back in with the Bees. I never knew what to expect from her.

With a flick of her wet head, Tara motioned to the other Bees. As one, they turned and jumped into the deep end of the pool. Whatever doubts Sonali might have had, they'd passed.

Gwen rose to her feet, sniffling.

"That must have been pretty scary," I said.

She nodded, tears still in her eyes.

I felt a tap-tap on my back. "Chrissa? Everything okay here?"

It was Dad, his eyebrows drawn up with concern.

I nodded. "Dad, this is Gwen. She had a little scare, but she's okay now."

"Well, that's good." He handed me a registration form. "I was able to get a new form at the front desk. It's signed. You're all ready now."

"Thanks, Dad. I'll see you outside after we're done," I said. Then I walked over to Liz, who was standing by Joel, demonstrating the sidestroke by reaching her hand toward the ceiling and snapping it down to her side. "Excuse me." I handed her the form.

"Yup, this puts you in my class." She glanced at the clock above the diving board. It was already 4:59. "Tomorrow," she said. "Today's session just ended. But, hey, nice job helping your friend just now. That was quick thinking on your part."

I nodded and then walked with Gwen into the locker room. I immediately moved my things from my corner locker to one next to Gwen's locker. I couldn't leave her alone to be stung again by the Bees. I expected them to say something mean, but instead they talked among themselves, just loud enough that I could make out their words.

"She wouldn't stop crying," Sonali said with a hint of genuine concern. "I thought she knew how to swim."

"Yeah," Jadyn murmured, "I mean, almost drowning would be scary, but carrying on like that? It was like she *had* to make a big deal out of it?"

"I think she was playing it up for attention," Tara said.

"I don't know," Sonali added. "I'm just glad she's okay now."

Chrissa

Lockers slammed shut and the voices drifted off.

"Don't listen to what they say," I whispered to Gwen, whose hair clung to her ears and forehead. She put on a quilted jacket with worn cuffs. It was thin and didn't look very warm. "Hey, aren't you going to dry your hair before you go outside?"

"I'm fine," she said.

"Do you need a ride home? We could drop you off—"

With a tiny yet firm shake of her head, she repeated, "I'm fine, Chrissa. Thanks anyway." Then she gathered her backpack, stuffed her wet towel into the bin, and headed out the door.

"I was just trying to help," I said to myself.

By the time I met up with Tyler and we rode away in Dad's truck, Gwen was already a block and a half from the center. As we drove past her, I waved out my steamed window, but she didn't see me. I hoped she lived close by, or her hair would freeze before she got home.

8

Magic Wand

When I walked into art class on Wednesday, rows of glazed bowls sat on the counter, waiting to be fired. They must have been from an earlier art class, and I guessed which bowl was Tyler's. It had to be the one decorated with all the planets in the solar system. Jupiter filled the inside of the bowl; on its outside, rings encircled Saturn, while swirls of green and blue formed Earth. He must have used a fine-tipped brush to paint Venus and Mercury. The colors were drab and muddy now, but I knew from watching Dad work that once the bowl was fired, they'd turn as bright as vibrant glass. Tyler's bowl was going to look great.

"Fifth-hour students," Ms. Rundell began as we took our seats, "have fun glazing your bowls today, but take your time. Use your utmost creativity! Make something you'd love to keep for yourself—but remember, these bowls will be part of the Sunrise House fund-raiser."

At my table, Gwen raised her hand.

"Yes, Gwen?"

"I don't feel well. May I go to the nurse's office?"

Chrissa

Ms. Rundell picked up her magic wand and dabbed at the air. "Of course, Gwen. May you feel better soon!"

Gwen had seemed fine earlier in the day when we worked together in the media center looking up facts on Alaska. Maybe she was getting sick from walking home with wet hair two days ago.

As Gwen slipped out of the classroom, Ms. Rundell instructed us to pick out bowls from one of several boxes. "Mr. Maxwell threw these bowls on his wheel and then bisque fired them." She explained that every piece of pottery is fired twice: bisque fired and then glaze fired. "The bowls you'll glaze, or paint, have already been bisque fired. Please handle them carefully. They're stronger than when they were greenware— before the first firing—but they'll still break if you drop them." As a potter's daughter, I knew that already, but I didn't say anything.

I turned over a bowl to find my dad's stamped imprint: *Maxwell Pottery.* Edgewater Elementary still felt like a foreign and dangerous land, so seeing Dad's imprint helped somehow. I liked that he was getting our art class involved with the fund-raiser. It was sort of like taking a thread of home and crossing it with a thread of school, the same way Nana weaves together different threads on her loom to create something new.

For a moment, I studied the bowl in my hands, wondering how to glaze it. The fund-raiser was to raise money to help people who needed a place of safety. I didn't like that I'd had to leave my old home and start over at Nana's, but at least I had a caring family. At least I had a safe home to return to at the end of each school day. When someone donated money to Sunrise House and in return got a bowl of soup—and the bowl to keep—I wanted that person to leave with a bowl that was cheery and full of hope, as a reminder that this donation was for a good cause.

From the plastic jars of glazes, I picked out Sunset Red, Passionately Purple, Orange Blossom, and Azure Sea Blue. With a pencil, I sketched my design on my bowl, and then I began to carefully paint my design with glaze. Ms. Rundell would fire as many bowls as she could in the art room's small, cylinder-shaped kiln, and Dad would swing by sometime during the day to pick up the rest to fire them in his studio. I love seeing pottery emerge from a firing, so maybe I'd go into his studio to help out tonight.

Minutes before the end of art class, Gwen returned. She sat on her stool and hid behind her bangs. I leaned closer. "Are you feeling any better?" I asked.

Chrissa

From the nearby art table, Tara cleared her throat and, as always, spoke in a voice that was just below the teacher's radar. "She was probably just faking it to get out of class."

Ms. Rundell announced, "Okay, class. We're out of time. Carefully set your bowls on the shelves as you leave. See you tomorrow!"

As students milled about, I spun around to Tara and the Mean Bees. It was one thing for *me* to get picked on, but it burned me to see her pick on Gwen again.

"I don't think Gwen would fake being sick," I snapped back. "But maybe you would."

Sonali's eyes widened, as if she was shocked that anyone would dare talk back to their little group's leader.

But Tara's eyes narrowed, as if she'd already started planning her counter-attack.

Jadyn piped up. "Maybe snobby rich girls should, like, mind their own business?"

I turned my back to them, held my tongue, and set my bowl on the shelf. Some of the bowls would undoubtedly crack in the firing. A tiny bubble trapped in the glaze or clay would burst in the kiln's intense heat. Being around the Mean Bees was like being in a kiln. They turn up the heat as though it is their job to see who will crack like a piece of broken pottery when some tiny bubble of weakness is revealed. But as much as I had already felt their pressure, I wasn't going to let them break me.

As I headed toward the door, I wondered why breaking someone made them happy. That's the part I just couldn't understand. Then I caught up to Gwen, tapped her on the shoulder, and asked, loudly enough for the Bees to hear, "Hey, Gwen, want to come over after school sometime?"

Gwen turned to face me. "Thanks," she said, "but . . . um . . . I can't."

I waited a second for her to explain why, but her lips were sealed. Wasn't she going to say something like "not this week, but maybe next week"?

Something more?

Sonali suddenly joined us and whispered, "Gwen, say yes. Chrissa has two stone lions at the end of her driveway and a really cool house."

I shot a glance at Sonali, who had just said something . . . *nice?* I didn't know what to think of her.

"C'mon, Sonali," Tara called. "Something smells like llama poop. She can't even make friends with the Loser Girl. Let's get out of here."

Chrissa

That afternoon at the pool, I hung out with Gwen in the last fifteen minutes of free time. I felt a little stung that she didn't show any interest in coming over to my house, but at least she acted interested in being friends at school and at the pool, despite Tara's comments.

With my goggles on, I demonstrated the "dead man's float" facedown in the water. I emerged after ten seconds. "Okay, your turn."

While she floated, I counted. ". . . eight, nine, ten."

She popped up, pushed her goggles back, and smiled. "I did it!"

"That was great!" I said. "You floated for ten full seconds!"

Just then, Tyler swam up to me. He had been over in the deep end of the pool near the Mean Bees. "Hey, Chrissa," he said, coming closer. I noticed Tara, Jadyn, and Sonali watching in the distance.

"What?" I asked, sensing that something was definitely up.

He came right up to me so that we were face to face, quickly hooked his finger in the noseband of my goggles, and snapped them.

"Ouch! Tyler, that hurt! Why did you—"

Before I could finish my question, he dove underwater and swam away.

I watched him glide through the water and climb up the nearest pool ladder just as the bell rang, signaling the end of practice.

I pulled off my goggles, bewildered. This was my *brother*. How could he do this to me?

I was used to an unexpected snowball, an occasional pillow that fell on me as I pushed open a door that was ajar, but this felt different. I was determined to get back at him, or at the very least, Dad would hear about it and Tyler'd lose privileges. I pictured the bowl he'd so carefully painted and imagined dropping it from a high cliff.

"That was mean," Gwen said.

"Yeah." As I rubbed around my eyes and cheekbones, which still stung, I glanced toward the diving board where the Bees were gathered. They were giggling as Tyler trotted off toward the locker room.

When they realized I was staring back, Sonali looked away first and headed for the locker room. Tara and Jadyn laughed harder together.

Now Tyler's prank made more sense. He hadn't

come up with that little trick all on his own. It smacked of Bee meanness. He'd been put up to it.

If I had a magic wand like Ms. Rundell's, I'd swirl it over the heads of the Mean Bees and say a few mumbo-jumbo words. Then *poof!*

They'd disappear forever.

9

S'mores

As Dad drove us home, I gazed out the back window. The days were growing longer, and the sun sent pale shades of rose and peach across snowy yards.

Dad glanced over from the wheel. "Looks like your art classes came to the rescue with the bowls."

"Yeah," Tyler said. "Mine's going to be so cool. I fit the whole solar system on my bowl."

"I figured that one was yours," Dad said. He tilted his head toward the back of the pickup. "I loaded up a few more kilns' worth while you guys were at swimming."

I didn't say a word. I was too mad at Tyler. He didn't deserve to be spoken to. Now I thought his bowl was the most stupid idea in the world. I mean, who puts a solar system on a bowl?

A space geek.

My brother.

The Pawn of the Mean Bees.

Dad pulled into Nana's driveway. I didn't know if I'd ever come to think of it as *my* driveway or *my* home. It just seemed as if it would always be Nana's and Grandpa's place, even though Grandpa was gone.

I pictured Grandpa only a few months back, lying in the hospital bed that had been rolled into the sunroom. His bed had side rails and a button for raising and lowering the mattress. In his last days, he seemed to see and do things that didn't make sense, such as talking to his own mother and father—my great-grandma and great-grandpa—who were most certainly long gone. But Nana had explained, "People close to death sometimes start crossing over into the next world before they're truly gone from this one."

Days before Grandpa died, I sat with him one afternoon while he slept. Outside the sunroom windows, the willow tree that had turned golden yellow rustled its leaves in the wind. The maples were painted bright shades of magenta and cranberry. When he woke from a nap, I took his cold fingers into my hands, trying to warm them. "Hi, Grandpa. Is there anything you need?"

His eyes, blue like mine, were brighter than usual. He looked at me intently and squeezed my hand. In a quiet voice, he said, "Just you, Chrissa Marie. All I need right now, in the whole wide world, is to hold the hand of my beautiful and precious granddaughter."

My eyes had filled then, and they filled again now, remembering him.

S'mores

Suddenly it was quiet. Dad had turned the engine off and the radio had gone silent.

"I'm starving!" Tyler said as he and Dad piled out of the truck.

For a moment, I just sat there in the back, too upset to say anything, too upset to move. Why did everything have to change? I missed Grandpa. I missed my old friends, and I missed how everything used to be.

I wiped away a single tear and then climbed out. As I headed toward the house, I gulped a deep breath of winter air. Slowly I climbed the front steps, scraped my boots on the doormat, and stepped into Nana's warm house.

After dinner, while Dad and Tyler worked together in the pottery studio, Nana suggested I do my homework in the sunroom. While she worked at her loom, I set my school library books on the craft table. It wasn't fair that Tyler didn't have homework. Not only did he have an easier teacher, but he was free from the Mean Bees. If he knew them better, he wouldn't be so quick to believe that they really liked him.

Chrissa

I stared at my library books, titled *Colorado, Rhode Island,* and *Florida.* Finally, I started skimming through them to find answers to the questions on my three-page worksheet, "All About States." Tomorrow we were supposed to work together in our clusters to share what we'd learned and help each other fill in the blanks. The last thing I wanted to do was share my carefully researched answers and give any help to the Bees. Of course, they were researching other states, too, and I'd get help from them. At least, that's how it's supposed to work. With the Mean Bees, I never know what to expect.

After a solid hour of studying, I packed my homework into my backpack. "Done," I announced.

"Good," Nana said, "because I think it's time for some s'mores. I'll start a fire in the living room fireplace, and you go get your dad and brother. Your mother should be home any minute."

I headed to the entryway, pulled on my jacket and boots, and darted out under a star-bright sky and into Maxwell Pottery.

The two-stall garage holds one large kiln, several potter's wheels—two electric and one kick-style—and aisles of shelves with pottery in various stages. The largest table is for kneading, wedging, and slicing clay.

In one corner, plastic bags of wet clay wait to be shaped into cups and creamers, pitchers and platters.

"Dad?" I called.

He and Tyler turned from the large kiln. "Hey, the first round of bowls turned out perfect!" Dad said, pointing at the kiln window. "Want to take a look? I can't open it yet, it's still too warm."

I walked over, avoiding eye contact with Tyler. I peered in. I could tell instantly that the bowls had not been painted by Dad. Some were splotchy with hardened drips, some were muddy brown from too many overlapping glazes, but some had turned out surprisingly well. A bright red bowl reminded me of something Asian. A white bowl with turquoise flecks was surprisingly pretty. And then I saw Tyler's bowl. It had turned out perfectly. The colors were bright and the planets actually resembled planets. I was still so mad at him that if I were Tara, I wouldn't have had a second thought about breaking his bowl! But I knew I couldn't do something that mean.

As we entered the house, the living room glowed from the fire that flickered in the fireplace, and the scent of burning birch logs filled the air. Nana had set out marshmallows, graham crackers, chocolate bars, and her secret s'mores ingredient—banana slices—on the coffee table. My anger toward Tyler almost softened.

I squatted before the fire, turning a marshmallow on a wire skewer until it was lightly golden. Tyler's went up in flames.

"Do you have to burn it?" I asked, breaking my vow of silence.

"The crisper the better," he replied.

Mom came home in time to join us, and for a few moments, life felt almost normal. She told us about one of the older male doctors who thought Mom was a nurse. "He asked me to get him a cup of coffee." Mom shook her head. "So I did. But I brought back *two* cups of coffee, and I set one on the counter in front of him and one in front of me. Then I said, 'Let me introduce myself, Dr. Tanner. I'm Dr. Maxwell, the new internist.' He was a bit flustered at first, but then we had a good consult over our coffee."

Along with my family, I laughed—and it felt good. Mom always has interesting stories from the hospital.

I placed my perfectly soft marshmallow on top of chocolate chunks and a graham cracker, slipped in a slice of banana, and then squashed another cracker on top. It was gooey and yummy, and I didn't care if my fingers were sticking together.

The hallway phone rang.

For a few moments, life felt almost normal.

Tyler jumped up. "I'll get it."

"Huh, that's not like him to expect a call," Dad said quietly to Mom. "Must be making some new friends."

"Yeah, she's here," I heard him say. "Chrissa! It's for you!"

I finished the last of my s'more, licked my fingers, and reluctantly walked to the hallway. I studied Tyler's eyes as he held out the phone to me.

"Who is it?" I mouthed silently.

He shrugged, but I didn't trust him. Something smelled as fishy as the dead carp that wash up on Nana's beach. And after Tyler's prank at the pool, I didn't know what to expect next.

He continued to hold out the phone. "C'mon, Chrissa. It's for you."

Reluctantly, I took the phone from his hand. "Hello?"

"Chrissa, it's me. Sonali."

I didn't bother to say anything. She had no reason to call me. We weren't friends.

"I want to apologize," she said.

"Is your mom making you again?" I asked, my voice pinched as I remembered her delivering the red bag.

"No, this is different. It's about what happened

at the pool today. I laughed when your brother snapped your goggles, but then in the locker room . . . well, I saw those red spots on your cheeks and I just want to say that it's not really Tyler's fault. We dared him. And it was *supposed* to be this big joke, but . . . it really wasn't funny."

"No, it wasn't." My grip loosened on the phone. Sonali was so hard to figure out. How could I know if she was being sincere?

"Today," Sonali continued, "I heard you ask Gwen over. And she said she couldn't. Well, I know you're not supposed to invite yourself over, but if you want someone to come over, well . . ."

Was she *asking* to come over? I could punish her by just telling her a flat "no." That would leave her wounded and embarrassed for asking. And it would serve her right. But on the other hand, if she was sincere and was actually trying to be friends, then I didn't know how to answer. "Um, let me think about it. I'll let you know tomorrow, okay?"

"I understand," she said, sounding disappointed. "Well then . . . see ya at school."

When I returned to the fire, I sat down by Tyler. He was roasting another marshmallow until it was blackened like soot. "Hey, nice marshmallow," I said.

"Thanks," he said quietly. "And hey, I'm really sorry I snapped your goggles. I don't know why I did it. It wasn't very nice."

I exhaled. "Just don't do it again," I said. Then I lightly punched him in the shoulder and his marshmallow accidentally dropped into the fire.

"Hey!" he said. "Why'd you do that?"

"How about we call it even?"

"Yeah," he said, nodding. "Fair enough."

10

Secret Notes

The next morning at school, Sonali slid her foot toward mine under our cluster of desks. When the side of her shoe touched mine, she withdrew and I placed my foot where hers had just been. All the while, I kept my eyes on my deskwork. After a moment, I stretched my arms up and then sideways and then down toward my toes, as if I needed to loosen up tight muscles. I found the tiny note under my shoe and, like a skilled magician—no magic wand needed—eased the note into my palm in one invisible motion.

I risked a glance at Tara and Jadyn. They hadn't seen a thing.

But I wasn't going to take any chances. I waited until lunch hour and let them get ahead of me going out the classroom door. Then I opened the note, which read:

Hi Chrissa!
I hope you'll say yes to my coming over after
school Friday. Don't breathe a word of this to
Tara. She'd be so mad!

Chrissa

The rest of the day, Sonali and I exchanged more notes. I told her I'd love to have her sleep over. Outwardly, she still acted like the other Mean Bees, as though my presence was a disturbance to the hive. Yet she seemed eager to be friends. In one note I suggested she ride the bus home with me, but she wrote back:

Not a chance! Tara and Jadyn ride your bus.
My mom can drop me off.
I'll bring my sleeping bag.

Passing notes right under the noses of the other two was like having a delicious secret. And I felt for Sonali. I knew how hard it could be to get caught in between friendships. More than once, I'd had to sort out friendship troubles back in Iowa with Amanda and Haley.

That night at home, I called Amanda and told her about school and how things were looking up with a possible new friend. "That's good, Chrissa," she said. "It was so hard for me when you left. I missed you—and still do—but it helped to start hanging out more with Haley."

When I hung up, I felt a little better, and yet sad, too. But when my cell phone beeped with a text

message from Sonali, my mood instantly lifted. Her
message read:

Cant wait to CU 2moro!!

When I hopped off the bus after school that Friday,
I barely noticed Tara and Jadyn's routine farewell.
"Bye, Tyler! We'll miss you! Have a good weekend!"
As I patted one of the lions, I realized that the
two Bees hadn't gotten to me. Maybe if Sonali was willing to be friends with me, then the Mean Bees didn't
have that much power. *Maybe*, I thought, *they have only
as much power over me as I allow them.* And this past
week, ignoring them had worked wonders. I continued
to be friendly with Gwen, but if she could never come
over, I wasn't sure we'd ever get close.
This time, when the black Jetta pulled into the
driveway, I met Sonali with a genuine smile. "Hi!"
She nearly danced around the car, grabbing her
overnight bag, a sleeping bag, and a pillow from the
backseat. She kissed her mom through the driver's
window and then skipped up the steps toward me.
"This is going to be fun!"
Looking up and down the long porch, Sonali
said, "This would be such a great place to play in the

summertime. Or to sit and read."

"In the summer, when I used to just visit my grandparents, I played out here all the time."

"And now you get to *live* here. It's so cool! I mean, Chrissa, it's like you live in a mansion!"

For a split second, my confidence and smile faltered. What if Sonali just wanted to come over because she liked Nana's big house? Did she think I was rich? Was that it?

"Chrissa," Sonali said, stopping as I opened the door for her. "I didn't mean it like that. It's a cool house, for sure, but that's not why I wanted to come over."

I needed to hear what she was going to say.

"I want to get to know you. Okay?"

I let out the breath I'd been holding. "Okay. It's just—"

"I know," Sonali said, stepping inside. "We got off to a bad start. My mom talked to me all about it on the drive over. When something goes wrong, it takes time to get over it. And I mean, with everything, I haven't been exactly—"

Her words hung there. "Forget it," I said, gesturing her inside. "Nana will holler if I let too much heat out the door. Let's take your stuff up to my room."

After going through a basic show-and-tell of my

room, we sat cross-legged on the floor with a few of my dolls. I learned that Sonali has two older sisters, who are both in college, and that her mom's parents came from India. She has a dog named Tofu that likes to eat toilet paper rolls. We laughed and then I told her how Keefer likes to take faucet-drip baths.

While I was giving Sonali a tour of the house, a hand-knit scarf hanging from a peg in the sunroom caught her eye.

"Did your grandma knit that from llama wool?"

"No," I said. "Um . . . I did. But that scarf is knit from sheep's wool."

She looked at me wide-eyed. "Is knitting hard?"

"No. It just takes practice."

"Could you teach me?"

"Sure!" And within minutes she was holding two wooden needles with a skein of blue yarn. Her loops were way too tight, but she was definitely getting the hang of knit and purl. I couldn't believe how much we already had in common. We'd barely gotten started, however, when Dad called from the kitchen.

"Chicken fricassee! Come and get the world's finest in home cooking!"

It was just the five of us—Nana, Dad, Tyler, Sonali, and me. Mom was still at the hospital.

Chrissa

Just as we started passing bowls and plates, all made by Dad, a phone buzzed from out of nowhere.

"Oh, that's my cell phone!" Sonali jumped up. "I left it in my coat pocket. I'd better check it."

If she'd grown up in my family, she'd know that answering phones during dinner is not allowed—unless it is the hospital calling Mom. Emergency calls only. All other calls, Dad always says, can wait.

My fork was midway to my mouth when Sonali returned. She stood awkwardly in the kitchen doorway, her shoulders twitching slightly. "Um, that was, uh, my mom. She's coming to pick me up."

"But why?" I asked. "I thought you were spending the night."

"Um, someone—I mean, our relatives are coming from out of town, um, for pizza. Sorry, Chrissa. I have to go. Sorry."

I went from feeling as light as a helium balloon to feeling the air *whoosh* out of me. "You're not kidding?" I asked, as I fell toward earth.

"Go ahead and eat," she said. "I'll go get my stuff and wait at the door for my mom. She'll be here any sec. Uh, thanks for the dinner, Mr. Maxwell, but I can't stay."

I stared at my plate. I couldn't believe it.

Then, before I knew it, the front door shut with

a *click* and a car's lights shone from the driveway.

"Well, that was odd," Nana said. "And here I thought you two were having such a nice time."

"She's not very good at lying," Tyler said.

I tried focusing on my food and bringing it to my mouth, chewing carefully so that I wouldn't choke. "Odd" wasn't the word for it—more like "suspicious." Either Sonali had lied, or she'd planned this all week long with the Mean Bees, getting my hopes up only to walk out on me when I was starting to feel safe. But then again, Tyler was right. Sonali *wasn't* very good at lying—or at being a loyal Bee. I still believed that she had truly intended to sleep over, but something had changed her mind.

I drank my milk in one long gulp and set my glass down with a *thud*. Everything about what had just happened stunk. There was only one *probable* reason why Sonali had lied.

It must have been Tara who'd called.

11

Disaster

With a little help, I managed to get through the weekend. Students and a few teachers showed up Saturday morning, as scheduled. The kids were interested in Dad's pottery studio, but Cosmos and Checkers were the biggest hit. When Sonali showed up and acted as if nothing had happened, I avoided her—like a bad case of the flu—by talking to other kids in the barn about the llamas.

When it was all over, I hid in my room for the rest of the day.

Sunday afternoon, when I sat down in the kitchen for milk and peanut butter cookies, Nana asked, "Okay, now that everyone's gone, what's with the moping around? You're spending so much time in your room, I barely see you. It's getting a little lonely in my sun-room. Even Keefer wonders where you've gone."

I shrugged.

"Maybe it didn't work out this weekend with Sonali. But have you tried to make friends with some-one who needs a friend?"

My throat felt hot. I couldn't tell Nana that I had

been in my room so much because I'd been crying. And I didn't want to start up again. Warm-from-the-oven cookies deserved better.

"Well?" she prodded.

"Nana, I've tried! Everyone has a group already. Most kids are nice, but it's not the same as being *real* friends, like with Amanda. And Sonali—well, she has *other* friends."

"Well, dear," Nana said, "don't give up."

Even Tyler tried to cheer me up. "Hey, Chrissa, we haven't played Brain Scan for a long time. Come on!"

Brain Scan is a game we made up. I joined him on the cushioned window seat in the living room. Keefer immediately hopped up and sprawled on his back between us for a belly scratch.

"Ready?" Tyler asked. "You start. Think of a color."

I had a hard time clearing my mind, but I pictured one solid color—orange. To hold the image more clearly, I imagined a real orange, complete with its puckered, shiny peel. "Ready," I told him.

He closed his eyes. "Is it orange?"

"You got it! Your first try!"

Tyler opened his eyes and clasped his hands over-head in a victory cheer. "Okay," he said, "my turn now."

This time I closed my eyes, trying to see the color

in his mind, but all I could picture were the Mean Bees. I made a lame guess. "Um, yellow and black?"

We've played this game ever since I can remember. It's surprising how often we know exactly what the other one is thinking.

"Nope," he said.

"Purple?"

"Try again. You're not concentrating, Chrissa." Sometimes Tyler sounds just like Dad.

I tried every color of the rainbow before we finally quit. "I give up."

"It's pink," he finally said. "I was trying to picture a happy color for you."

At school, I survived halfway through the week by becoming a turtle and pulling myself into an armored shell. Even the Bees couldn't penetrate it.

I was glad when we had art class. It was my only real break from being near Sonali and the others.

"Class," Ms. Rundell called out. She motioned toward the bowls on shelves. "Between Mr. Maxwell's kiln and our kiln here at school, all the bowls are now fired. We lost only two, which is quite miraculous. The fund-raiser on Saturday should be a huge success because of your artistry and your willingness to help out. You've made a real contribution, and I'm proud of all of you!"

Then she instructed us to get started on our next project, which involved going through boxes of magazines to clip out images that demonstrated an interest of ours.

"Anything we want?" someone asked.

"Whatever interests or delights you," she answered. "Now, I have to go to the office for a minute, and when I return, I expect you'll all have found some inspiration."

I focused on llamas. But after flipping through a few magazines, I hadn't found a single image. Gwen didn't seem to have the same problem. She immediately cut out an image of a woman playing a harp.

"Do you play the harp?" I asked.

She shook her head. "No, I just like harps. I used to play the violin. I don't have one anymore."

I wanted to ask her what happened to it, but she hunched down again in serious concentration. That's when I came across an image of a girl with bangs cut above eyes as round and big and dark as Gwen's.

I inched it across the table right in front of her.

"She looks like you," I said. "But your eyes are even prettier."

With the back of her hand, she brushed her bangs away from her eyes. "Think so?"

"Absolutely. I don't lie," I said a little loudly, hoping Sonali might hear. Then I whispered, "I have a bunch of barrettes you could borrow if you want to try clipping your hair back. It would show off your eyes more. They'd work great while you're growing out your bangs."

"I'm not growing them out." She sighed. "My mom just hasn't had time to trim them. I keep asking her, but she's always—" She glanced at my blunt safety scissors. "Hey, you could trim them."

"*Me?*"

Her suggestion startled me, but then, with all the fabric I've cut to make doll clothes and crafts, I have a pretty steady hand. I studied her bangs. They were feathery but cut pretty much straight across. It couldn't be that hard, and it would take only a few seconds.

"Gwen," I offered, "if you come over sometime after school—I mean, if you can—then I could try."

"You could trim them now," she said.

"Now? Here? That doesn't seem like a good idea."

Disaster

"Well, not *here*."

Ms. Rundell was still gone, so we slipped into the girls' restroom. I wasn't sure that trimming bangs at school was a good idea, but then, Gwen wasn't planning on ever coming over to my house.

We stood beside the sinks and mirrors.

"Okay, just face me and close your eyes," I said. Though I felt a little nervous, I was glad to do something helpful. I know what it is like to have a mom who gets way too busy at times. When Mom did her residency as a doctor, she worked eighty-hour weeks. Some weeks I barely saw her. But that was a few years ago, and she'd had to learn everything then—even surgery. Compared to surgery, what was a little hair trimming?

I picked up my scissors. "Ready?"

Since I'm left-handed, I started at the left edge of her bangs.

Snip. Snip. Snip. I watched as less than one-fourth of an inch of hair dropped to the floor in tiny flecks. I tried to be really careful. Any quick bump could turn a haircut into a disaster.

Just then, the restroom door swung open. "Look! It's a beauty salon," Tara called.

"Just keep going," Gwen whispered.

As Tara walked over to us, I stopped cutting and withdrew the scissors.

"My mom owns three hair salons and spas," Tara said. "I don't mean to butt in, but I know something about hair."

Gwen's eyes snapped open.

Jadyn now stood near Tara, and Sonali hung back near the door, watching.

I held the scissors behind my back. "Leave us alone," I said, keeping my voice calm.

"No, really," Tara said, standing at my shoulder. "I've watched my mom, like, a hundred thousand times. To trim bangs right, you need to twist the ends like this—" She demonstrated by pulling her hair over her shoulder and twisting the ends. Then she made scissors motions with her fingers. "Snip lightly. That way you'll get a more natural-looking cut. And it's faster, too."

"Are you sure?"

She whispered, "Otherwise it will look like you put a bowl over her head."

"Gwen," I said, "close your eyes again."

At first she squinted suspiciously, and then she closed her eyes tight.

I studied the results of my hair-dressing skills so far. Where I'd cut, the ends of Gwen's bangs *were* blunt.

They were so blunt that it looked as if I'd chalked a line and cut straight across—almost as if I really *had* put a bowl on her head and cut along its edge.

"I'm telling the truth," Tara said. "Let me show you."

She held out her open hand.

I didn't budge.

"I don't know . . ." I stammered. But if her mom owned salons, Tara definitely knew more than I did about trimming bangs. I mean, I'd never cut anybody's hair before.

Maybe I was making a big mistake, but with more than a little reluctance, I put my scissors into Tara's outstretched hand.

Without saying another word, Tara lifted Gwen's bangs gently, twisted them just as she'd demonstrated, and snipped the ends lightly. *Snip!* She lowered them and looked at her work approvingly. I had to admit it; the bangs did look more natural. Then she lifted Gwen's bangs again, as if to touch them up, but instead used the scissors to hack off Gwen's bangs—short and jagged—in one fast motion. *Snip!*

As the scissors clattered to the floor, Gwen opened her eyes wide.

"Nice job, Chrissa!" Tara exclaimed. "Gwen, you

really *do* have pretty eyes."

Giggling, Tara and Jadyn fled. Sonali stared at us but then turned away, too, and slipped out the door.

Gwen faced the mirror and brought her hand to her forehead. "Chrissa! How could you?" Her face crumpled into tears.

"But I didn't," I started. "It was Tara!"

Gwen's bangs were jagged and terrible looking. I didn't know what else I could do or say. It was too awful. And Gwen thought I'd done that? I felt as if the wind had been knocked out of me. Shaking, I reached down and picked up the scissors and a few snips of Gwen's blonde hair from the floor . . . wishing there were some way to undo what had just happened.

Heels clicked on the restroom floor. "What in the world—?" came Ms. Rundell's voice. Hands on her hips, she looked pained as she took in the scene. Even though I knew I wasn't fully guilty, somehow I'd allowed this to happen. I knew I should speak up and tell Ms. Rundell about Tara and her latest prank—but I couldn't get a word out.

"Chrissa Maxwell!" Ms. Rundell said. "What have you done?"

12

Principal's Office

As the hallways emptied and students caught their buses home, I waited with clammy palms outside the principal's office for Dad and Mom. The door to Mrs. Ziminsky's office was shut, and I sat in the waiting area along with the Mean Bees and their parents.

Earlier, Gwen and her mom had met with Mrs. Ziminsky, Mr. Beck, and Ms. Rundell. From my classroom window, I'd seen Gwen leave school early.

Tara's mom's hair was as feathery as a well-groomed show dog's, and her bangs, I noticed, were cut perfectly. In a silky gray jacket and skirt, she crossed and uncrossed her legs, reapplying her red lipstick twice in the span of ten minutes. "Tara," she whispered, "I know you didn't do anything wrong. Don't worry."

She patted Tara's hand as if she were a toddler and then turned Tara's hand in her own. "But honey, your cuticles are awful! As soon as we're done here, I'll get you in to see Anna to get you touched up."

Tara dipped her head, leaning into her mom's shoulder—a picture of sweetness. But when her mother glanced the other way, Tara flashed me a confident and smug "I'm-not-worried" smile.

Across the room, Sonali sat between her parents. Her father rested his folded hands over his striped tie (his nails would probably pass Tara's mom's inspection). Sonali's mom adjusted the brightly colored wrap that she wore over her black turtleneck sweater and then opened her purse. Sonali looked my way as if to tell me something, but I couldn't read her eyes. How could I when she was always switching sides?

Near the door, Jadyn stood with her dad, a bald, thick-necked man in a denim shirt and jeans. I wondered if Jadyn had helped him lose all his hair. He wore an expression that said he didn't have time for this.

When Mom and Dad arrived, the woman behind the desk lifted the phone. "They're all here now."

Then the door to Mrs. Ziminsky's office opened. "Thank you all for coming in so quickly," the principal said, and she pointed to a nearby conference room. "We'll meet where there's a little more room." Once we were all settled at the long table, Mrs. Ziminsky pushed her glasses higher on her nose with her forefinger and then gazed around the room. "Something terrible happened to Gwen Thompson this afternoon, and girls, you all seem to have some involvement or knowledge of what happened. And it seems that you three girls—

Tara, Jadyn, and Sonali—have gained a reputation for bullying other students. We need to get to the bottom of all of this and put an end to it. What happened to Gwen today is totally unacceptable."

"This is ridiculous!" Tara's mom blurted. "My daughter is bright and hardworking, and she is not the kind of girl who goes about causing trouble."

Tara sat tall, with a look of bewilderment on her face. "I wouldn't hurt anyone intentionally," she said.

Mrs. Ziminsky held up a note. I recognized it instantly. It was the valentine addressed to Gwen. "What about this?" the principal asked. "Who wrote it?"

"Well," Tara said, looking around to the other Mean Bees—and me. "We all did, really. In our cluster. It was just supposed to be funny, not meant to hurt anyone. A joke. We were, well . . ." She shook her head with false regret. "I guess we weren't thinking."

The principal lowered the valentine, as if her evidence didn't amount to much now. "Girls," she said, "I want to know who cut Gwen Thompson's hair in the restroom today."

"Chrissa," she began. "You go first."

I glanced at Mom, who was still in green scrubs, and Dad, who'd come over so fast from his studio that flecks of clay still clung to the tops of his hands. They were watching me intently. I cleared my throat, sat on my trembling hands, and told the principal how every-thing had gone wrong and how Tara had been the one to cut Gwen's bangs.

Tara's mom *harrumphed.* "Oh, I don't believe a word of this! Who's to say you're not lying?" She glared at me.

"I'm telling the truth," I said, looking at Mom. "I want to be friends with Gwen. I wouldn't do some-thing mean like that."

"As if my daughter would?" Tara's mom blurted out again. "Is that what you're implying? Tara," she said, "honey, you tell them what really happened."

Tara wore the innocent expression of someone who had been wrongly accused. She said that she had given me some tips on how to cut bangs and that I had just gone ahead and ignored her and hacked them off unbelievably short. "That wasn't what I'd meant at all. But I realize that, well, the only place to get hair cut is at a salon, like one of my mom's. We should have known better. I should have gone to get the teacher when Chrissa started to cut Gwen's hair. But I thought I could help."

My mouth dropped open. How could someone be so good at lying? She could win an Academy Award for her performance, which Mrs. Ziminsky seemed to soak in. "Okay, thank you, Tara. Now Jadyn?" Mrs. Ziminsky said.

Jadyn's version of the story ended with, "All I know is that when I looked again, Gwen's bangs were cut really short and, like, Chrissa was holding the scissors?"

Jadyn's dad clapped his large hands together. "Okay, good," he said. He nodded at Jadyn.

When the principal looked away, Jadyn flashed Tara a secret smile.

So far, it was two against one. And since Gwen hadn't spoken a word to me since the hair-trimming incident, I didn't know what *she* thought had happened or what she'd told the principal. As far as I knew, she may have told Mrs. Ziminsky that *I* was the one who had cut her hair. And why wouldn't she think that? I was the one she'd last seen holding the scissors.

"Sonali?" Mrs. Ziminsky continued.

If Sonali didn't tell the truth, then I was doomed. I imagined myself hobbling away in a striped prison uniform, with shackles around my ankles.

She looked straight at Mrs. Ziminsky. "Um, I don't really know what happened. When I entered the girls' room, it all happened so fast that I didn't see."

"You didn't see?" Mrs. Ziminsky prodded. "You're sure?"

Sonali nodded and then studied her lap.

Mrs. Ziminsky's glasses had slipped down again. She pushed them up with her forefinger, looked around the room, and then leaned forward on her elbows. "Bullying is a real issue," she said, "and we've been too lenient about it in years past. What happened today is *not* acceptable and will be dealt with. For now, I thank you parents, especially, for taking the time to come and meet together this afternoon. I'll keep you posted on where we go next with this incident and issue."

Tara's mother redid her lipstick and said, "There's no need for me to return with Tara. We all heard what went on. I'm finished here—and so is my daughter." She stood up. "Come on, sweetie."

The room cleared quickly, except for my parents, who had been so unbelievably quiet. Why weren't they saying anything? It wasn't until Mrs. Ziminsky stood that they spoke up.

"Thank you," Dad said, "for taking this kind of thing seriously. I remember all too well as a kid being taunted and teased. It's not funny at all. We're grateful that you're looking into this. And we obviously have a lot to talk about at home." He rested his hand heavily on my shoulder, as if he were the jailer ready to lead me away. My own dad didn't believe me!

When I stepped outside the school and walked toward the truck, I cried, "Dad! You acted like I'm guilty! How could you?"

"I don't know what to believe yet," he said. "You know I love you no matter what. And I know you have a good heart. But, on the other hand, you've been acting different lately, so I don't know . . . Someone wasn't telling the truth in there, and parents who say their kids could *never* be guilty *always* seem suspicious to me."

Mom reached for my hand, but I pulled away. "Mom, you could have defended me! You and Dad didn't say a word!"

"Like Tara's mom? Is that what you wanted?"

Dad started the engine and I just stared out the window. I didn't want my parents to pretend I was perfect. That wasn't it. I'm not sure what I wanted from them. I supposed they would ground me for the weekend, but it wouldn't matter. I had no friends. No one was going to invite me over anyway.

The whole way home, I wanted to feel sorry for myself. But the person I couldn't stop thinking about was Gwen. I felt *terrible* for her. There was no way she could hide what had happened. Every time she looked in the mirror, she would think of how someone had been mean to her. I couldn't change what had happened.

But no matter what she thought, I had to find a way to make it up to her—to make things right with her.

The next morning, I still felt terrible. My head hurt from everything that had happened, and my stomach was in about a thousand zillion knots. I buried my head under my pillow, wishing away another school day.

"Knock, knock," came Mom's voice at my door. "May I come in?"

I groaned and then answered, "Oh, okay."

"Aren't you getting up for school?" she asked.

"Mom, I just can't." I shifted onto my elbow. "The thought turns my stomach into a washing machine."

Although she was clearly ready and dressed for work, she settled onto the edge of my bed as if she had all the time in the world. "It's Friday, then the weekend. Think you can make it just for today?"

I wanted to tell her exactly what had been happening at school since my first day at Edgewater. Holding it all inside was killing me. Instead I said, "Mom, is it okay to take a sick day when your heart and head really, *really* hurt?"

She rested her silky, cool palm on my forehead.

"Hmmm. You do seem a little warm to me."

"I do?" I said with a little too much enthusiasm.

She nodded gravely. "Yes, I'll call and ask your teacher for your assignments and pick them up for you so that you don't get behind."

"You will?" I rested back on my pillow with relief. I wasn't going to have to sit with Cluster Four today. And I could put off facing Gwen.

Mom continued, "Although I don't usually recommend this remedy for most of my patients, I think I know exactly what you need to start feeling better."

"You do?" Now I was a little bit worried. If I wasn't really sick, taking medicine could be a bad thing.

"After you went to bed last night, your dad and Nana and I were talking about tonight's fund-raiser at the Community Center. We think—"

"That's tonight?" I'd completely forgotten.

She nodded. "And Nana thought it would be an extra-special touch to have the llamas there. Remember how Nana and Grandpa used to take their old llamas to nursing homes? Everyone loved them. Anyway, with this particular ailment of yours, I think that helping Nana get Cosmos and Checkers groomed and ready is just what you need." She smiled at me. "I think I'll help, too. But it's up to you. What do you think?"

"But don't you have to go to work today?"

"I'm thinking that I'll clear my schedule for the day."

"You will? Why?"

"Just because. Besides, there's a new batch of interns in need of practice. They'll fill in for me. Now, Chrissa, there's only one condition to your being home today."

"What's that?"

"I want you to tell me *everything* that's been going on at school. Come on—let's sit on the window seat."

I wiped a tear from my eye, and then the dam broke and I started sobbing. Mom gave me a bear hug and just held me, letting me cry out all my hurt and pain into her shoulder. She waited until my sniffles lessened. Then she handed me a tissue and I blew my nose with such a loud snort that we both started laughing.

And then I told Mom everything, starting with the stolen valentines and teasing, all the way up through the haircut disaster.

"Oh, Chrissa," Mom said. "You shouldn't ever have to put up with this nonsense. Bullies come in all shapes and sizes—and ages. I remember being teased for getting top test scores when I was your age."

"You were?"

And then I told Mom everything.

"I never told anyone, either. It almost made me want to try failing school instead of getting good grades. I thought that if I dumbed down, others would like me more. But then I realized how stupid that would be. I'd only be hurting myself."

"So what'd you do?" I asked.

"Well, I just kept doing my best and ignored the rest. Plus I found some friends who liked me for who I was. But guess what?"

"What?"

"Even now I sometimes have to stand up to other adults. Adults who think it's their job to make someone else's life miserable. They feel better about themselves when they put someone else down. Bullying doesn't happen only with kids."

"So will we tell the principal—and Gwen—what really happened?" I asked.

"Absolutely. I'm just sorry that you've been trying to figure all this out on your own. The important thing, though, is that you finally spoke up and told the truth." She looked at me intently. "Now, don't you think it's time to say, 'that's enough'?"

I practiced the words in my head and then let them roll off my tongue. "That's enough," I said. "That's enough!" I repeated. And this time I meant it.

Mom smiled.

"I'm feeling a little better already. But Mom, if I tell, won't I be tattling?"

"Honey, you're *telling* in order to protect yourself and others. You are reporting what happened, which is the right thing to do. If you were tattling, it would feel different—more like you were trying to hurt someone else's reputation somehow. Do you see the difference?"

"I'm not sure."

"Tattling means bringing someone down out of meanness. As I see it, you're telling, not tattling. By speaking up, you're going to help put a stop to something that's wrong. Can you do it?"

I nodded. All I had to do was picture Gwen's cruel haircut.

For the first time in days and days, I was filled with energy.

13

A Good Cause

At 9:30 that morning, I returned to school with Dad and Mom for an appointment with Mrs. Ziminsky.

"Well," I began, knowing that I had to speak out, even though I was scared. I cleared my throat. "It pretty much started on my first day at Edgewater." Then I told her everything from start to finish. My chin trembled at times and I thought I might start crying, but telling the second time was a little bit easier. And with each telling, I felt stronger somehow, too.

"Thank you, Chrissa," Mrs. Ziminsky said, resting her chin on the tips of her steepled fingers. "Thank you. It takes a whole lot of energy to hold in this kind of hurt, and when we finally tell the truth, it can leave us feeling a little raw and exhausted. I agree that a day at home is more than warranted. I'll meet with your teachers today, and we'll take it from here."

As we headed to the parking lot, Mom squeezed my hand and Dad patted my shoulder. "We're proud of you," he said.

At home, I flew through my homework. After lunch, Mom, Nana, and I groomed Cosmos and Checkers until their winter coats looked perfect. When we were done, I poked my head into Dad's studio. "The llamas are ready for the big event, Dad."

"Good," he said, turning from the deep sink, "because I could use a little help washing these bowls. The glaze is safe to eat from, but I'm worried that people will choke on the dust."

We washed, dried, and packed up bowls for the evening's fund-raiser. I was glad to be busy, because every time I stopped to think, my stomach flip-flopped. Although I'd told Mrs. Ziminsky what had happened, I really didn't know how things would be now. Was Gwen even at school today? No doubt the Mean Bees would lie again and deny everything—and not even Gwen knew what had happened because her eyes had been shut.

As soon as Tyler hopped off the bus, we all piled into Dad's truck and Nana's van, which were filled with bowls and llamas, and headed for the Community Center. "I thought you didn't feel well," Tyler said as we unloaded the llamas at the Center.

"I feel better now," I replied. There would be time later to fill him in.

We helped haul boxes into the center's large kitchen and stacked bowls on the end of the serving counter, which held large, steaming pots of different kinds of soups and stews. They smelled so good, my stomach grumbled.

Mr. Beck was in the kitchen in a red apron, slicing loaves of bread. "Chrissa!" he called. "Glad to see you made it!"

I waved to him. "Let's go get the llamas," I said to Tyler. I guessed that Mrs. Ziminsky and Mr. Beck had talked, and I didn't want him to ask me about the Mean Bees right now. My newfound confidence was still a little shaky. In fact, I hoped the Bees would not show up at all.

As more people arrived, Tyler and I formed the "greeting committee" inside the main doors. I held Cosmos by her lead rope, and Tyler held Checkers.

"Llamas!" a little girl chimed. She pulled at her mother's arm. "They're little!"

"That's because they're mini llamas," Tyler said.

"May she pet them?" the mom asked.

"Sure," I replied. "One child at a time."

Soon, I was so busy answering questions about llamas that—to my relief—I didn't see everyone who came through the doors. Before I knew it, Dad came out to find us. "Okay, almost time to start. Let's settle the llamas back in the van for now."

A Good Cause

When Dad, Tyler, and I returned, the tables and benches were filled with families eating and visiting. I was relieved not to see the Mean Bees. We quickly found Nana and Mom and sat down with them.

My family. My safe zone.

A man in a V-neck sweater and tie stepped up to the small stage and microphone. "Good evening," he said. He explained that he was the director of Sunrise House. "Every donation made tonight will directly benefit Sunrise House, which serves families caught in emergency situations and in need of housing." After a short talk, he concluded, "This event wouldn't have been possible without Maxwell Pottery, and extra help from the fourth- and fifth-grade students and teachers of Edgewater Elementary. Please stand so that we can thank you!"

As we all stood up, the room exploded with applause. The director continued, "These fourth- and fifth-grade students and their teachers and parents deserve your applause, because not only did they help decorate the bowls, but they'll also be washing them for you to take home."

Another round of applause floated up.

"And now, I'd like to introduce a person who has become a dear friend and who is willing to share her

story . . . willing because she wants to help us understand the purpose of and need for Sunrise House.
Please welcome Janine Thompson."

From a table near the front, a woman about
Mom's age stepped up to the stage, leaving a girl sitting
alone. From the slump of the girl's shoulders and the
back of her blonde head, I knew it was Gwen. I couldn't
see her face or her brutally short bangs, but something
stirred in me. I couldn't let Gwen sit there alone. Before
I knew it, I was walking past tables and heading toward
her, my heart chugging like a train gaining speed. Then
I sat right down on the empty bench beside her.

Her eyes seemed even bigger under her stubble
of bangs as she glanced over at me.

"Hi," I mouthed silently.

Gwen's mother had started talking. "This rose
I wear," she started, indicating the red rose on the lapel
of her blazer, "is the symbol of Sunrise House. Roses,
I've discovered, can indeed grow in the midst of thorns.
Though it's extremely difficult for me to share my story,
I've been asked to help give you a picture of why your
donations are so important, so needed."

Next to me, Gwen clenched her hands together
so tightly that I thought she'd cut off her circulation.
I reached over and gave her hands a quick squeeze.

A Good Cause

I was relieved when she squeezed back—and then held on.

Gwen's mom went on to explain how her family had fallen on hard times when her now ex-husband lost his job. Despite her job as an office manager, they lost their house when they were unable to keep up with payments. "Then I woke up one morning to learn that my husband had left us, and my daughter and I were evicted—truly homeless. It happened that fast. I always thought homelessness happened to *other* people. Never to me. That was late last fall. At first, my daughter and I slept in our car.

"I'd park so that we'd wake up near a wayside rest area or a restaurant—somewhere where we could use the sink for washing up—and then I'd go to work and pretend that life was just as it had always been. But I wondered what we'd do when winter came along." She paused. "I was too ashamed to ask for help. And then the first snows fell. We buried ourselves under blankets, trying to stay warm in the car. Barely sleeping, even though we were exhausted. Finally, when all seemed lost, we found help through the caring staff at Sunrise House. Without Sunrise House, I don't know where we'd be today."

The room was completely still. Now I understood

why Gwen had washed her face at the school sink.

My heart broke for her. I had complained about having to change schools and living in Nana's house instead of our own, but I'd never considered what it would be like to be without any roof over my head.

Suddenly, Sonali—of all people!—slipped past me and sat down on the other side of Gwen. Out of the corner of my eye, I watched her. Though she looked straight ahead at Gwen's mom, out of her pocket she pulled a paper napkin on which she'd written something. She handed it to Gwen, who unfolded it. I saw what Sonali had written:

I'm so sorry. Please forgive me.

This was something I had never expected.

As Gwen's mom spoke, she explained how, with help, she and her daughter were putting their lives back together again. She smiled as she announced, "And just last weekend we left Sunrise House and signed a lease for a nearby apartment. It's small, but honestly, *home* never looked so good. Most importantly, we have hope again. Thank you."

When she finished, the whole audience stood up and applauded.

A Good Cause

Afterward, Gwen, Sonali, and I worked together clearing tables.

"Gwen," Sonali said, stacking dirty bowls on a tray, "I hope you know that it was Tara, not Chrissa, who cut your bangs. Chrissa wouldn't do something like that."

I placed a fistful of spoons on a tray and turned to Sonali, thankful that she'd backed me up.

"I know." Gwen stopped wiping a table. "The principal told us earlier today what really happened. So thanks. But, um, Sonali? Aren't you friends with Tara and Jadyn?"

Sonali shook her head in slow motion, as if she had given the subject plenty of thought. "Not anymore. I've been friends with Tara since we were in preschool. Tara's always been a little bossy, but this year it got worse, and, well, I didn't know how to say no to her. But when she cut your hair, Gwen, I finally realized that things had gone way too far. When I said I was going to tell, she threatened to make my life miserable if I didn't back up her version of the story, but you know what? I don't care anymore. And I'm sorry that I was ever mean to either of you."

"Wow," Gwen said. "I think you mean it."

"Thanks, Sonali," I added, hoping that her change of heart would last. This time, it seemed it might. And there was a whole weekend ahead to find out.

"Hey," I said, brightening the mood, "can you two come over tomorrow?"

Gwen's eyes glowed. "Now that you know my secret and that I can ask *you* over someday, too, the answer is yes!"

"Sure," Sonali beamed. "I'd really like that."

"Good, because I have a really cool idea. It'll be fun!"

14

Solidarity

On Monday morning, when the bus picked Tyler and me up from the end of the driveway, everything felt different. For starters, it wasn't just Nana's driveway anymore. It was *our* driveway—*our* home—*our* lions watching over the realm. And it wasn't just a new school anymore. It was *my* school now.

I hopped on the bus, proudly wearing my new headband. Over the weekend, Gwen, Sonali, and I had worked for hours in the sunroom making headbands. We'd stitched up the edges of fabric squares, folded them, and then decorated them with sequins, buttons, and embroidered ribbon.

"Hi, Tyler!" Tara called out as we climbed the bus steps and took our seats. "Have a good weekend?"

"Yeah, it was okay," he replied, sitting down beside me. He flipped open his newest library book, *Wonders of the Universe.* Even if Tara and Jadyn still tried to get to me through Tyler, it wasn't working.

As agreed, I met Sonali and Gwen outside Room 103 before class started. We stood together in solidarity, wearing our headbands, as planned. Each was unique, but with all three of us wearing them for the rest of the year, I hoped Gwen wouldn't feel so self-conscious as her bangs grew out.

When Tara and Jadyn neared the classroom, they shot us poisonous looks and paused in front of us. Tara scrunched up her nose. *"Eeew!* Something stinks!"

I ignored her.

"And Sonali?" Tara asked, crossing her arms and cocking her head. "What's that on your head?"

"Yeah," Jadyn joined in, "are you guys trying hard to look stupid?"

"Take it off, Sonali," Tara said, almost under her breath, "or you're out of our club."

A brief cloud of pain drifted across Sonali's face. I worried that she was going to once again cave in. But she pressed her shoulders back and said, just as she'd practiced at my house, "No. I'm not taking off my headband. I like it. Besides, we had a great time making them this weekend at Chrissa's house."

"Whatever," Tara said, pivoting toward the classroom. Jadyn followed at her heels.

"Mr. Beck," I said, stopping him as he hurried toward the classroom door. "We need to talk with you. We want you to do something."

"Can it wait, girls? Class is just about to start."

Solidarity

Sonali shook her head. "No, I have to say this while I'm feeling brave. And we need your help."

"Okay then," Mr. Beck replied, closing the classroom door. "Make it quick."

In the quiet hallway, Sonali explained again what had really happened with Gwen, how bad she felt—and how she wanted to start over.

"I see," he said. "And the headbands?"

"They're to show Gwen we support her and to show everyone that we stand up for others," I said. "We can make more, too, if other kids want them."

He nodded. "Okay. You know that the principal is in the process of formulating school policy to address issues of bullying. That will take some time, but for now, what do you want *me* to do?"

I spoke up. "We'd like to rearrange the clusters so that we can sit together."

"Hmmm," he replied. "Given the circumstances, that's not too much to ask."

As Mr. Beck opened the door, we gave each other a thumbs-up and headed inside. Sonali and I sat down at Cluster Four.

Tara scoffed. "What was that all about?"

"You'll see," I answered.

The moment school announcements were over,

Mr. Beck stepped to the front of the room. "Before we get started today, I've decided to make some changes in seat assignments."

A few groans went up from the classroom.

"But I like where I'm sitting," someone complained.

Mr. Beck held up his forefinger. "Gwen, please trade desks with Jadyn."

"What!?" Jadyn's eyes flashed green. "This isn't fair."

"But Mr. Beck," Tara said sweetly, sitting tall in her seat. "Remember, you let us choose our clusters in January."

"And Tara," he continued, "you will trade with Joel in Cluster Number Two."

Tara's eyes narrowed, and she whispered, "He can't do this. I'm going to tell my mom."

No one budged.

"Let's move *now*, people," Mr. Beck stated. "For the rest of you, this would be a good time to take a few minutes to clean and organize your desks while we wait."

My desk hadn't had much time to get messy, but I lifted the desktop and moved around my pencil and marker containers anyway.

Tara yanked out her textbooks and notebooks

and dropped them to the floor.

Bam!

"Pick those books up," Mr. Beck ordered, "and try that again. Quietly this time."

Tara obeyed. Then she leaned around the edge of her desk and whispered to me, "This is all *your* fault."

"I don't think so," I whispered back.

"You're going to pay," she added, "for stealing Sonali." Then she went back to emptying her desk.

In less than ten minutes, Tara and Jadyn were separated and relocated to new desks in different clusters. As Tara sat down, another girl in her new cluster pulled a stretchy headband out of her backpack and put it on. She flashed me a quick grin as she adjusted it in her hair.

With the two Mean Bees gone and Gwen and Joel added, Cluster Four had taken on a whole new look and feel.

"Hey, I don't mind being in this cluster," Joel said, "but I'm not wearing one of those." He pointed at our headbands.

Sonali, Gwen, and I laughed.

"Don't worry," I said. "We won't make you. It's a free country."

And for the very first time since I'd started at Edgewater Elementary, I felt ready to be part of my new school.

Change, I realized, can be a good thing.

Letter from American Girl

Dear Readers,

　　We receive thousands of letters from girls every year. From these letters, we know how hard it can be to stand up to bullies and, unfortunately, how often bullying happens. We wrote Chrissa's story to show how one fictional girl learns to handle some difficult relationships—and to inspire you as real girls to find ways to handle challenging people in your own lives.

　　One way to put an end to bullying is to keep the conversation going. Read the following real letters from real girls who are looking for ways to stand strong when dealing with bullies. Get together with others who have read Chrissa's story, and talk over the discussion questions on pages 130 and 131.

　　Keep trying. Keep talking. Together we can make a difference.

　　　　　Your friends at American Girl

Too Scared to Speak Out

Dear American Girl,
There's a girl who goes to my school, and she's different. I try to be her friend, but my other friend is really cruel to her. I'm too scared to stick up for her.
—Scared

You know in your heart what you need to do. The next time your friend is cruel to this girl, be brave and say something like, "Why don't you just leave her alone?" Don't pass up the chance to do what's right because you're afraid of a bully. You won't feel good about yourself, and you might miss out on a new friendship, too. You can also give the heads-up to the teacher, so she can keep an eye out for the bullying and put a stop to it.

To: American Girl
From: A victim
Subject: A rotten girl

Dear AG,
There's a girl in my class who often comes up to me surrounded by friends and says with a smirk, "I think you're really pretty." I know she's being rotten, but I guess she thinks I'm too dumb to figure out that she means the opposite. How do I deal with her?

You need to let this bully know that you understand what's going on. One way to do that is to look annoyed and walk away. Another way is to look her in the eye, use her exact same tone, and say, "Thanks, I think you're really nice." You have to act very confident for that to work, though, so you may want to practice at home in front of a mirror or with a parent. Also, know in your heart that one of the things this girl doesn't have is inner beauty, so hold your head up and let yours shine.

Been There! Done That!

Dear American Girl,
A mean girl at school won't leave me alone!
My mom says, "Just try ignoring her." Been
there! Done that—about 20 times!
—Miserable

It takes nerves of steel to tune out someone who's deliberately tormenting you. And it may not stop this girl. If ignoring is going to work, it will work in the first week or two. If the bullying continues past that, you need a new plan. Keep track of what she says and when she says it. Get support from your parents and teachers. You can also try letting her know that you want her to LEAVE YOU ALONE. Let her know that if the bullying doesn't stop, you'll have to report her to the principal. Then, if need be, do just that.

BF Bully

Dear AG,

One of my best friends is kind of a bully. I know I shouldn't be friends with a bully, but I've been friends with her for a LONG time. I know why she acts like that—it's because she doesn't get a lot of attention at home. When it's just me and her, she's great, but when we're around others, it's like she's a totally different person. I wish I could get her to stop.

—Frustrated

Have you tried talking to her? She may not realize she acts so differently around others. When the two of you are alone, let her know how much you appreciate the nice side of her. But also let her know that it hurts your heart to see her be mean to others. When she is being mean, be sure not to join in—and stand up for others when you can. Also, if she has told you she misses her parents, encourage her to talk to them and let them know she needs more family time.

Hot and Cold

Dear American Girl,
I have a "hot and cold" friend. One week, we'll save seats for each other, play at recess, and tell each other secrets. Then, the next week, she won't talk to me, she says mean things behind my back, and she lies to me. I want to be her friend, but she is too unpredictable. Help!
—On-and-off Friend

Your friendship sounds like a toxic one! You need to have an honest talk with this girl the next time she tries to freeze you out. Let her know that it's bully behavior and that you are not willing to put up with it. Then don't. Put some distance between the two of you, and put energy into other relationships. By doing this, you might be able to still be friends, just not as close as before.

To: American Girl
From: Afraid
Subject: Bullies

Dear American Girl,
The boy next door always kicks me and pulls my hair. I'm afraid if I fight back, he might hurt me even more. If I tell his parents, he'll get punished, but he'll still beat me up. What should I do?

Putting your hands on someone else in anger—or otherwise—is serious. You should report this, fast. Talk to your own parents first. They can talk to this boy's parents or come with you when you do. You also need to stop playing or interacting with him for a while. Try not to go near him and ask that he not enter your yard. This boy may never be the ideal neighbor. But if he knows you won't cover up for him, he'll think twice before he hurts you again.

Discussion Questions

1. Chrissa had many chances to talk to adults about what was going on, but she didn't. What makes it hard for a child to go to an adult when he or she is being bullied? What do you think Chrissa was afraid of? If she had talked to an adult, would it have changed things? What would you do?
(pp. 25, 35, 47, 54)

2. Throughout the story, Sonali appears to be torn between listening to Tara and listening to her heart. Why do you think Tara had so much power over Sonali? What does that say about their friendship? What would you have done if you were Sonali? Have you ever been stuck in the middle?
(pp. 65, 84, 115)

3. Initially, Tyler didn't understand that he was being pulled in and used to bully Chrissa. When do you think he started to understand what was happening? How do you think he tried to "make it right" with Chrissa? When you make a mistake, how do you heal things? *(pp. 16, 66–67, 77–78, 87–88)*

4. Chrissa wasn't able to stand up to the mean girls until they tricked Gwen into coming into the deep end of the pool. Why do you think she stood up for Gwen then? Is it easier to stand up for someone else than it is to stand up for yourself? How do you think it made Chrissa feel to speak out? Have you ever stuck up for a friend? *(pp. 57, 59, 107)*

5. When it comes to relationships, we learn a lot from our parents. What did you think of the way Tara's mother acted? If you had to choose, which mom would you want, Tara's or Chrissa's? Why? *(pp. 98, 104, 106)*

6. *Solidarity* means to stand together for the same purpose or cause. How do you think Gwen felt when her classmates wore headbands? If you were in the class, would you have worn one? Why or why not? Have you ever joined with others in a cause *you* believe in? How did it make you feel? *(pp. 117, 119, 122)*

Meet the Author

Mary Casanova has published more than twenty books, including *Jess* and *Cécile: Gates of Gold,* also for American Girl. To write *Chrissa,* she tapped into her own childhood memories, as well as drawing on her experiences as a parent of two children who are now in college. She and her husband live in northern Minnesota, where they ride their horses, Midnight and JJ, and explore Rainy Lake and Voyageurs National Park with their two dogs.